"Good morning, angel," Matt said, pulling a rose from his lapel.

Susan's gaze was caught by his fingers twirling the flower. She tilted her head and stared into his mysterious eyes. Her gaze lowered to his lips. What would it be like to be kissed by that incredible mouth?

He traced the rose along the sensitive curve of her jaw. Her spine seemed to melt. Unable to resist, she glanced up and was trapped by the intensity in his dark gaze. She felt the faint erotic pressure of the flower petals massaging her parted lips.

As Matt lowered his head, she instinctively swayed toward him, wanting to be touched, to feel the way only he could make her feel. She closed her eyes, and in the pleasure of darkness came the caress of his lips. Cool satin. Searing heat. Desire spiraled along her nerve endings.

Then the school bell rang, and reality hit her. She pulled away, but Matt wove his fingers through her hair and wouldn't let her go.

"Don't do that," she said firmly.

"Don't do what?" he asked. "Don't touch you? Don't kiss you? Don't want you?"

"I don't neck with strangers in the parking lot."

"We haven't been strangers since we met. I know you, Susan. I've dreamed you. And that kiss was just a beginning. . . ."

WHAT ARE *LOVESWEPT* ROMANCES?

They are stories of true romance and touching emotion. We believe those two very important ingredients are constants in our highly sensual and very believable stories in the *LOVESWEPT* line. Our goal is to give you, the reader, stories of consistently high quality that may sometimes make you laugh, sometimes make you cry, but are always fresh and creative and contain many delightful surprises within their pages.

Most romance fans read an enormous number of books. Those they truly love, they keep. Others may be traded with friends and soon forgotten. We hope that each *LOVESWEPT* romance will be a treasure—a "keeper." We will always try to publish

LOVE STORIES YOU'LL NEVER FORGET
BY AUTHORS YOU'LL ALWAYS REMEMBER

The Editors

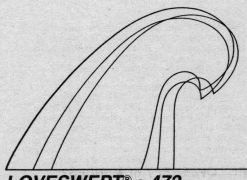

LOVESWEPT® • 472

Theresa Gladden
Romancing Susan

BANTAM BOOKS
NEW YORK • TORONTO • LONDON • SYDNEY • AUCKLAND

ROMANCING SUSAN
A Bantam Book / May 1991

*If you would be interested in receiving protective vinyl
covers for your Loveswept books, please write to this address
for information:*

Loveswept
Bantam Books
P.O. Box 985
Hicksville, NY 11802

ISBN 0-553-44123-X

Published simultaneously in the United States and Canada

*Bantam Books are published by Bantam Books, a division
of Bantam Doubleday Dell Publishing Group, Inc. Its trademark, consisting of the words "Bantam Books" and the
portrayal of a rooster, is Registered in U.S. Patent and
Trademark Office and in other countries. Marca Registrada.
Bantam Books, 666 Fifth Avenue, New York, New York
10103.*

PRINTED IN THE UNITED STATES OF AMERICA

OPM   0 9 8 7 6 5 4 3 2 1

For Rich and Jenni, who make living a true joy.

Deepest gratitude to Lisa Cantrell, whose talent, encouragement, and generous spirit inspires me.

Special thanks to Sue Maly for reading the manuscript and laughing in all the right places, and to Dr. David Call for his invaluable help.

Romancing Susan

One

The old witch still scared her to death.

Susan Wright sped toward Brownstone Elementary School. Tension and self-directed irritation dulled her previous enjoyment of the spring day's pleasant warmth. A single hive formed a blotch on her neck. Just thinking about being in the same room with crabby Abby Riggs frazzled her nerves, transformed her from a successful—oh, did she ever love the sound of that word *successful!*—and confident businesswoman back to a squirming, guilty ten-year-old.

Knowing she was going to be late made matters worse. The hive itched like a severe case of poison ivy. Telling herself to chill out didn't help. She cast a wary eye out for cops, then urged her aging station wagon to exceed the speed limit another notch.

Why wasn't the old lady dead? she wondered as she glanced again at her watch. She pictured Mrs. Abigail Riggs sitting poker-stiff behind her desk, stern gaze fixed upon the clock, lips pursed tighter than the steel-gray bun knotted on top of her birdlike head, planning every word she'd say to her less-than-prompt ex-student. Susan hesitated at a stop sign, then turned the corner. She really didn't wish her dead, but retirement would be nice.

Think positive, she told herself. She'd be calm and assertive. Mrs. Riggs would not make her feel like a kid today. No, Susan would walk into the room and— *the Crab would go for her throat.* Oh, yes, she was positive about that.

Susan looked once more at her watch and winced. The hive begged to be scratched, but she kept her hands firmly on the wheel. She tried to think of a good excuse for being late. Clients giddy with spring fever wouldn't cut it. She had enjoyed their idle chitchat, but most of them had kept her far past their allotted time. Still, Abby Riggs, who didn't believe in idle anything, wouldn't care. She'd have to think of something better. She gave up. Nothing short of death—her own—would be acceptable. What a lousy Wednesday!

The red-brown-brick elementary school came into view. Susan's grip on the steering wheel relaxed. In spite of her feelings about her former fifth-grade teacher, she smiled fondly at the stately three-story building. It looked like an early nineteenth-century girls' school, built when high, vaulted ceilings were the rage and heat was cheap. She remembered how the long corridors served as delightful echo chambers for a swarm of laughing, shouting children. Brownstone Elementary remained a well-kept institution in Millers Creek, North Carolina. It was a rock, sturdy and steady, and no doubt would stay that way forever.

Unlike some people, she thought, and in particular a certain ex-husband.

Sturdy and steady.

That was what she wanted from life. Safe and secure. Just like Millers Creek itself: population somewhere near ten thousand, slow to change, and no unpleasant surprises.

Susan slowed down and drove into the school's circular drive. A group of kids played softball on the lawn. She noticed one small boy whose legs hugged an oak tree branch while he hung upside down. His wide grin and outstretched arms seemed a welcome to the April sunshine. Three girls jumped rope on the sidewalk. She recognized the singsong rhymes they shouted with each high swinging arc. It was good to know some things never altered.

She scanned the compact parking area. It was full except for one space close to the entrance. The neighboring church was holding some kind of meeting, and they were making use of the school lot as well as the entire street. Susan made a face at the idea of wedging the wagon in a tight parallel spot. It was a drag, but she'd do it or die.

Taking a deep breath, she maneuvered into proper driving-manual position, then slowly backed in. She hit the curb with a good two feet of automobile left to squeeze between a Toyota and a van.

"Damn!" Judging distance wasn't her forte. She'd been the only teenager in driver's ed to flunk the test three times for knocking over those stupid barrels.

The hive on her neck burned with frustration. Her eyes took on a stubborn gleam. She'd parallel-park if it took all afternoon. Old Crabby would deliver the same lecture if she was two minutes late or two days late. So what the hell.

Susan eased out and lined up again. In the rearview mirror she noticed a white sports car zipping up behind her and courteously decided to wait until it passed. Besides, parallel parking was difficult enough without onlookers.

The sleek little number didn't pass by. It slid without effort into *her* space.

"Oh, no." She scowled at the other driver. "No, you don't." Her palm slammed against the horn. Throwing the gear in park, she flung open the door and hopped out.

Matt Martinelli removed the key from the Jaguar's ignition, reached for his briefcase, and wondered what he'd done to make the lady in the station wagon mad. Opening the door, he uncoiled his six-foot body and got out. He shut the car door with a light touch of his hand, all the while watching her march toward him like an avenging angel.

He didn't consider himself the greatest connoisseur of women, but he knew what he liked. And he *liked* those nice legs coming at him. Her bold stride spoke of athletic grace. The body accompanying the lovely limbs was tall, well-proportioned, and shamefully encased in a no-nonsense black and white, business suit.

She stopped a foot or two shy of him. Great legs, he amended to himself. His gaze slowly inched up from the hem of her straight skirt. Her face wasn't bad either. Not classically beautiful, but quite pretty. She tilted her head back and fixed him with an unfriendly stare from blue-gray eyes.

Matt smiled. "Is there a problem?"

Frost gathered in those eyes. "You bet there's a problem." Her hands snaked up and rested on her hips. "That's my parking space. I was here first." Wind picked up a strand of her shoulder-length honey-blond hair and whipped it across her face. She impatiently shoved it back. "This happens to me way too often and—"

"You're mad as hell and ain't gonna take it no more." He gave her his best grin, the sale-of-the-century variety.

"—and it pisses me off," she continued, unaffected. "You're in my space."

"Did you call ahead to reserve it?" he teased. Legs to die for, he thought appreciatively, and a voice to match. This lady's vocal cords generated more heat than a steam engine. Move over, Kathleen Turner!

Susan didn't respond to his attempt at humor. She looked him up and down. Heaven save her from sexy, charming men, she thought with faint hostility. "You stole my parking place. I was lining up to parallel-park and you came barging in. I would appreciate it if you'd move that Tinkertoy elsewhere."

Intrigued by the voice and awesome legs, Matt entertained a fleeting thought of leaning closer and planting a kiss on her appealing lips. That image was followed by another, of her fist connecting with his nose. He'd discovered Millers Creek to be a friendly town, but he didn't think this particular resident was in the mood for the kissing-cousin routine. Since he couldn't go with his fantasy, the least he could do was give her a lesson in recognizing classic cars. "This"—he gave the Jag a loving pat—"is not a Tinkertoy. It's a Jaguar. An XKE." She didn't appear to be impressed, so he added, "It's a classic."

She gave the automobile a cursory glance. "Big hairy deal. I wouldn't know a classic Jag from a crying jag. All I care about is it's in my way."

He laughed. "I'm sorry. I honestly thought you were leaving. I'll find somewhere else to park." *In an hour or so*, he added silently. He knew he should make a quick exit, but the urge to stay was stronger. He wanted to listen to her speak again, wanted to see her smile, wanted to know her name, and he most definitely wanted to know if she was busy tonight.

"Why aren't you moving?" she demanded.

"I will. But I have to be truthful, though. You don't have a Popsicle's chance in hell of cramming that station wagon in this small space."

She bristled. "Yes, I do."

Matt shook his head. "Not unless it folds up like an accordion."

"That's my concern." Not for the world would Susan admit she was having a few doubts along the same lines. She was simply standing up for her rights. There'd been a time when even pushy salesclerks intimidated her, but not anymore. Her wimp days were over. In the midst of self-congratulations, she realized the hunk with the "classic Jag" still wasn't moving. She wished she could see his eyes, hidden behind don't-give-a-damn Ray-Ban sunglasses. With his olive complexion, she'd bet they were hazel. She gave herself a mental shake. What did the color of his eyes have to do with anything? "What are you waiting for?" she asked impatiently. "You're making me late."

"I was just thinking I owe you an apology. Why don't you let me buy you a cup of coffee? We'll get acquainted and I'll show you I'm not your ordinary no-good-parking-space-thief kind of guy."

His attractive grin was hard to ignore. Susan deliberately focused on the top of his head and found herself fascinated by the way sunlight made his hair look blue-black. She tried to resurrect more hostility and roused only curiosity. "Are you trying to pick me up?"

"Yes. How'm I doing?" His grin brightened a kilowatt.

"Terribly," she said, smiling back. If that sensuous grin on his full lips could be bottled, she thought, somebody would make a billion or two.

"Okay," he said. "How about, 'you're adorable when you're mad and I'd love to get to know you'?"

She shook her head. "Worse. That line went out of style with high-button shoes. Not even my great-aunt Dellie would fall for that one."

Who was this crazy man? she wondered. She was certain she'd never seen him around town before. The way his stonewashed jeans hugged his hips and legs like a jealous lover was something she'd have remembered. The sport jacket over a black T-shirt with a red silk-screened bow tie at the neck was a rather strange combination, and most of the men she knew wouldn't dare let their hair touch their collar. The handsome and expensive leather briefcase he negligently stowed on top of the car didn't fit his clothing. She stared at the red and aqua Converse sneakers on his large feet. Did he really expect her to take him seriously?

"Do you think," he asked, "your great-aunt would

fall for 'what's a nice girl like you doing in a place like this'?" He flashed her another one of those outstanding grins. Susan decided he'd perfected the art. He could bring strong women to their knees with it.

"No, she would not. I don't have time for this," she said, feeling more exasperated with herself than with him. Indulging in flirtations with strange men wasn't her style. He was attractive enough to tempt the wings off a choir of angels, but for all she knew he might be somebody's husband. That thought annoyed her. Oddly enough, she didn't want him to be the kind of married jerk who hit on women in parking lots. "Would you please move your . . . classic Jag?"

Sighing, Matt reclaimed his briefcase. "How 'bout, 'this must be my lucky day because I've just met the loveliest lady this side of the Mason-Dixon'?" He liked the way her hair floated around her face when she shook her head. "No?"

He opened the car door and tossed the leather case onto the passenger seat. "Do you come here often?"

She gave him a peeved look but he could tell she was trying not to smile.

"Yes," she answered, "every day at two-fifteen. I give my ten-year-old daughter a ride home." The smile finally materialized as she delivered her coup de grâce.

"Of course," he mumbled, "all the best legs are taken."

"I beg your pardon?" she asked, eyeing him suspiciously.

He leaned against his car, folded his arms across his chest, and pointedly inspected her ring finger. "Then I suppose the station wagon and child comes with a husband?"

"That's right," she lied, "a great big one, built like a defensive end for the Miami Dolphins. He eats for breakfast raw meat and people who annoy me."

One black brow arched above the sunglasses. "You aren't wearing a wedding ring."

Susan flushed. The eyes behind the Ray-Bans didn't miss a trick. "It's at the cleaners." She lifted her chin, brazening out the ridiculous statement. Let him think what he wanted as long as he packed his tempting smile back into the Jag and got out of her way.

He laughed. The rich sound disarmed her, making her forget her intention of moving him along. "I was right," he said. "You're adorable, but you're not a very good liar. Am I making you nervous?"

"No. Why?"

"You've got a big red blotch right there." He reached out to touch her.

The long, tapered finger he drew gently along her neck produced a shocking tingle of awareness. Susan felt like she'd been hit by a bolt of lightning. Her eyes widened in disbelief as pure energy seemed to radiate between them. She watched an amazed expression spread across his face and knew he'd experienced something similar.

He slowly withdrew his hand. "Incredible. Life is certainly full of surprises, isn't it?"

She recovered her composure. "I don't like surprises. Please move your car. I want you to move it now or I'll call the police."

"What are you going to tell them? Someone stole your parking place?" His mouth twitched with laughter.

"No," she said ever so agreeably, "I'm going to tell them you were speeding in a school zone and endangering the lives of children."

"You wouldn't."

"Yes." She smiled. "I would."

"I guess that means you won't have coffee with me."

"Right."

"Okay. It's been a pleasure." Tipping an imaginary hat, Matt reluctantly slid into the Jaguar. He was confident he'd see her again. Millers Creek wasn't Chicago. It was only a matter of time before they'd run into each other somewhere. And if it didn't happen soon enough, he'd memorized her license plate, and would beg or bribe the necessary information out of the appropriate authorities.

Susan walked back to her own car and got in.

The Jag pulled up alongside her. Matt leaned over and rolled down the passenger window. "What's your name, angel?"

Responding with an unconscious smile, she waved him away, then put the wagon in reverse.

While Susan attempted a second try at parallel parking, the man's knock-'em-dead grin remained in her mind's eye. Why was she always attracted to men whose behavior leaned heavily on the outrageous, nonconformist side? Hadn't she learned anything being married to Brian? Men who marched to the beat of a different drummer were strictly taboo. She'd sworn off such men along with her musician ex-husband.

As she backed into the spot, she hit the curb again with the front end of the automobile sticking out at an odd angle. Mentally repeating a vow to avoid parallel parking—and strange men who were anything but stable and steady—she whipped out for another try.

The freckle-faced boy abandoned the oak tree and walked over to her. He began shouting eager directions to her. "Turn your wheels to the left. No. Too far, too far. Whoa!" To her embarrassment, other children deserted their activities and gathered around. Some giggled. One yelled for her to get a horse. She wished she'd never seen the blasted parking space, but refused to admit defeat.

On her fourth effort the Jaguar man walked by. He smiled an I-told-you-so smile, blew her a cheeky kiss, then strode on into the school. Another hive popped up on her forehead.

Deciding to give up before she turned into a walking mass of red blotches, Susan headed back to the street. She left the wagon parked a block away and ran.

"Old Crabby Abby, that's my teacher, is ticked off. Says if my mom doesn't show up soon, she's gonna cancel the conference. That's okay by me. She's going to tell her I'm not doing so well in math—and that'll make my mom crazy 'cause she's an accountant—and that I talk too much. Do you think I talk too much? I don't think I talk too much. Mandy talks a whole lot more than I do, but Crabby Abby never catches her. Do you think that's fair? I don't think it's fair at all. Did I tell you my name? It's Nikki. Actually, it's Barbara Nicole Wright, but everybody calls me Nikki."

Susan heard her daughter's voice long before she saw her. It joyously rebounded off the walls, echoed down the long hallway, and met Susan around the corner. She sighed and wondered who Nikki was spilling her guts to. Like great-aunt Dellie, the little girl was interested in everyone she met. Her friendly habit didn't frighten Susan because she knew Nikki had her share of street-smarts, but that didn't stop the girl from chatting a willing ear off whenever she considered herself to be in a safe place.

"My mom's name is Susan . . ."

Susan grimaced and walked faster.

". . . and my dad is Brian. He's a musician and . . ."

Just name, rank and serial number, Nik! Susan wanted to yell.

". . . he doesn't live with us anymore. We're divorced. I don't like being divorced."

As she practically sprinted down the corridor, Susan wondered where she could buy a kid-size muzzle.

"I haven't seen him in a long time," Nikki went on. "He travels with his band a lot. Don't ever get divorced," the girl sagely advised. "It's not much fun."

Susan rounded the corner and saw her fair-haired child leaning against the wall outside the principal's office. She froze. Her heart rate accelerated. Smiling down at her daughter was the Jaguar man.

As Matt gazed into the sincere big blue eyes staring up at him, he felt a pang of empathy for the little sprite. She reminded him of his sister Cara at the same age. Worldly wisdom and a bit of cynicism peeking through childlike trust and innocence. What made a man abandon his family? he wondered. He'd raged over the same question thirty years before. He still didn't have an answer.

At the sound of approaching footsteps, the child glanced past him. Frowning, she said, "You're late."

Matt turned, and a crooked smile formed on his face as the appealing woman with the great legs stopped beside the little girl. "Barbara Nicole Wright's mother, I presume?" he said.

She nodded, and he wondered why a blush rose to her cheeks. "I'm Matt Martinelli." He extended his hand.

"Susan Wright." Susan's palm tingled as his olive-colored hand swallowed up her paler one. The sensation rapidly spread to her fingertips. Once again her accustomed air of command took an unexpected hit to the midsection. He maintained the contact a fraction longer than necessary, then let go.

"Crabby Abby is sooo pissed at you, Mom," Nikki said.

Her gaze returned to the child. "That's not a nice thing to say. Where did you learn that word?"

"What word?" Nikki asked innocently.

"Pissed."

"From you."

A suspicious sound emitted from the Jaguar man, and Susan glanced up at him. She noticed the

Ray-Bans were gone and his eyes were not hazel. They were deep, heavenly brown. Almost black. Her breath caught in her throat. Gypsy eyes. In them she saw admiration mixed with laughter, though he maintained a bland expression.

In her peripheral vision she caught Nikki watching her and the Jaguar man with undisguised interest. Gathering her parental dignity, she admonished her daughter. "Well, that isn't a nice word. I'll try not to say it anymore and *you* are not to repeat everything I say. Got that, kiddo?"

"Yes, ma'am."

Matt repressed a chuckle. Although the little girl had responded properly and respectfully, her impish face said she knew her mom wouldn't remember to stop using that word and neither would she.

Susan sighed. "I've also warned you about talking to strangers." She made the mistake of looking at the Jaguar man again. He grinned, reminding her at once of his effect on her hormones as well as her guilt of committing the same offense not ten minutes before.

"Susan Wright!"

The shrill voice lashed out into the hall, wrapping itself around Susan's nerve endings. She paled and slowly turned.

Several classrooms down and across the hall, Abigail Riggs stood in an open doorway. "You are *tardy.*" Disapproval formed a tight line upon her thin lips.

Once again laughter rose up in Matt's throat, and he forced it back. The old gorgon made lateness sound equivalent to murder.

"You always did dawdle about in the corridor talking to your friends or daydreaming," Abigail Riggs went on. "I had hoped adulthood would change such habits in you. However, I am very disappointed to realize time and experience have not taught you better." She gestured for Susan to accompany her into the classroom. "Come in. I have much to discuss with you. You've wasted enough of my time. I would think your child's welfare would be of utmost concern to you, and would ensure your promptness."

"Yes, ma'am," Susan responded automatically. Wearing a chaste expression, she began walking down the hall toward the teacher.

Matt looked on in disbelief. Was this the same woman who'd practically told him to get the hell out of her parking space? Surely, she wasn't going to meekly obey the old bat's autocratic order? But he remembered her response to his asking about the hive on her neck. And he remembered his pinch-faced, stiff-rumped third-grade teacher, Sister Annadell. Maybe Susan's reaction wasn't so strange after all, he thought with sympathy. If, heaven forbid, he came face-to-face with the ruler-wielding five-foot nun today, she'd probably still have the power to make him quake in his shoes.

Just when he thought the lovely-legged Susan Wright was going to slink off in disgrace, she stopped. She drew herself up as if she'd suddenly regained her backbone. Atta, girl, he thought, grinning encouragement. Let 'er rip.

"Mrs. Riggs," she said firmly, "you're absolutely correct. We do need to talk. I, too, have a great deal to discuss with you."

Susan glanced back over her shoulder. The Jaguar man gave her an approving smile and a thumbs-up, which she returned without thinking. Then she zeroed in on her daughter. "Nicole, go to the library. I'll meet you there when I'm finished. And I expect to see you doing your homework."

Matt silently applauded her proud, head-held-high entrance into the old bat's cave.

Chuckling softly, he gazed down at Nikki. She was staring at him with her young-old eyes as though she were sizing him up.

Seeming to come to some decision, she said, "Sometimes my mom acts a little weird, but I like her anyway."

"So do I," Matt answered.

Two

The next day—Thursday—Matt sat alone in the upstairs parlor of the Millers Creek Historical Society. He slowly turned the pages of a leather-bound scrapbook, pausing here and there to read the captions neatly typed under yellowing photos. Through the history preserved by the society, he discovered how the town had begun as a tobacco-farming community, then slowly evolved into a textile-mill town, thanks to the river and the railroad system. Old photographs from the late 1800s showed downtown Main Street had changed little in the past hundred years beyond the obvious modern updates.

He looked up when he heard footsteps in the hall, then smiled as Susan Wright walked into the room. Gone was the no-nonsense business suit. She wore a feminine dress in celestial blue. With her blond hair for a halo, she looked like an angel—one preoccupied with earthly things, judging from the way she concentrated on the papers in her hands.

"Good morning, angel."

Startled, Susan looked up and lost her grip on the tax forms she was perusing. They scattered to the floor. His brown eyes crinkling with amusement, the Jaguar man stood up and walked toward her. A thousand butterflies tried to take flight in her stomach.

"I didn't mean to frighten you," he said.

"Oh, well, I didn't realize anyone was up here." She knew Millers Creek was too small not to run into him again sooner or later. But this was the last place she'd expected to see him. She lowered her gaze, away from the Gypsy eyes and pirate's smile she found much too attractive.

They bent down at the same time to pick up the papers and bumped heads. Stars briefly swam in her vision. Hands wrapped around her upper arms, drawing her upright.

As her vision cleared, she saw his compelling gaze rove over her face. He stood so close she could almost feel the strength and heat of his body. The awareness she'd experienced with him the day before returned in a dizzy rush.

"I'm sorry," he said. "Are you all right?"

"Fine. No problem." Her head was fine. It was her reaction to him that concerned her.

"Allow me." He gathered the forms and held them out to her.

"Thank you," she said, absently rubbing a hive forming on her wrist.

"Are you certain you're okay? Sit down for a moment."

"No. Really, I'm fine," she protested as he guided her toward a green velvet love seat by the window. Feeling a little foolish, she sank down. As he sat beside her, Susan wondered why she had to keep running—literally—into this particular man.

The air seemed almost to sizzle as they sat silently gazing at each other. She liked his face, she mused. It had a well-used quality, showing years of living and humor around the eyes, nose, and forehead. She noticed his Roman nose had been made imperfect by a long-ago break, yet it didn't lessen his rough-edged beauty. He projected an aura of elemental masculinity, though he seemed entirely unaware of it. He also wore his clothes with careless ease. He was dressed in the same style as the previous day, in jeans and two-toned high-top sneakers. Only today he sported a Mickey Mouse T-shirt under his jacket.

"So, what brings you to the Historical Society?" she asked when she could no longer bear the silence or the undercurrent flowing between them.

He flashed his pirate's grin. "Research."

"For what?"

"I'm gathering historical background for a promotional video I've been commissioned to do on the area to attract new industry."

Her eyes widened in disbelief. "You're doing the chamber of commerce film?" From what Nikki had told her the night before, she'd thought he just owned a video rental store and took on simple taping jobs.

He nodded. "That's the one."

"But I thought a professional company out of Winston-Salem, was being considered for the project." The promotional film was vital to their community, she thought. Surely the chamber of commerce wouldn't take a chance on an amateur?

"They were," he said, "until I gave a presentation on my work and underbid the competition."

Embarrassed, she admitted, "I was under the impression videotaping was just a sideline of your video store. Someone told me you had been hired to tape student-teachers at Brownstone Elementary."

Amusement flickered in his eyes. "My store, Reel to Real, is a separate venture from my film production. I'm new in the business, but I'm not an amateur. I studied film at the University of Chicago."

"A degree in film," she murmured, impressed with his credentials regardless of her personal reservations about him.

"No. I have a degree in business. I took film courses because the subject fascinated me. By the way, I'm flattered you were interested enough to inquire about me."

"Nikki told me," she said dryly. "She talked about you constantly last night. You and your video store are big hits with her. She adores movies."

"She's a great kid; the kind who can take up residence in your heart before you know what's happening."

Susan realized the note of pleasure in his voice was genuine. She smiled. "You like children."

He nodded. "I enjoy looking at the world through their eyes. Everything is new and exciting to them." He grinned self-consciously. "I'm a sucker for anything small and helpless. If you want to see a grown man get goofy, just show me a baby or a puppy."

"Brian liked babies too. He just didn't want to be responsible for one." As soon as the words left her mouth, Susan regretted them. She never offered such private information to strangers.

"Your ex-husband?" he asked.

She nodded reluctantly.

"Then he, was a fool. You were wise to dump him."

Though he'd spoken softly, the intensity of his tone surprised her. She suddenly sensed Matt Martinelli was a complex man, a man a woman could spend a lifetime with, peeling through the layers.

"Do you like movies?" he asked.

"I used to," she said, smiling in gratitude for the change in topic. "But I don't have much time for that sort of thing."

"What do you have time for, Susan Wright?"

The gleam in his eye was more provocative than she could handle from this man. Smoothing a nonexistent wrinkle from her dress, she answered firmly, "My family and my work. And speaking of work, I'd better get back to it. Have to stay on schedule, you know." She braved a glance at him. His smile brightened the room, sending her pulse on a marathon.

"I understand you're a CPA." He glanced at the forms on her lap. "Working on the society's taxes?"

She nodded. "It's my way of volunteering my time to the preservation of our history."

"A busy CPA who volunteers her time for a good cause. I like that." He cocked his head to one side. "Want to be my accountant?"

Thinking about working in proximity with him produced a near anxiety attack in Susan. She needed to be his accountant about as much as she needed to jump out of an airplane with an umbrella for a parachute. "I'm sorry, but I'm not accepting new clients." She couldn't believe she was turning away business, but taking him on would be a conflict of interest—he was much too interesting and she didn't want him to be.

"I'm sorry too." A broad grin spread across his face. "I was looking forward to your examining my assets."

Was her temperature rising or was it merely warm in there? she wondered. The cheeky man wasn't speaking in terms of credits and debits, and he knew she knew it. She answered lightly, "What if I discovered your liabilities outweighed your assets?"

"I have no doubt you could find a way to improve my assets. We could discuss it over coffee."

The offer was tempting. He was tempting. But the less time she spent in his company, the safer she'd feel. "No. I really must go now." She rose in a fluid movement.

He met her refusal with a smile, but the gleam in his eye challenged her. "Perhaps another time."

Susan backed away. "Well, I'll let you return to your research. I apologize for disturbing you, Mr. Martinelli."

"You do disturb me, angel," Matt said softly when she was gone, "but I don't mind at all." That was an understatement. Her image had remained with him while he'd given his video presentation to the principal of Brownstone Elementary School the day before.

There had been a time when he'd been so entrenched in business, nuclear fallout wouldn't have fazed him if it occurred during a meeting. "Yes, indeed," he said aloud. "Life is definitely full of intriguing surprises these days."

The next evening Susan took her family out for their ritual Friday night dinner at The Red Dragon.

"He's really nice, Mom," Nikki said as they crossed the parking lot, continuing an ongoing monologue. She bounced just ahead of her mother and great-aunt Dellie, executing a new jazz step she'd learned in dance class, then walking backward.

Susan shot her daughter a warning look. Matt Martinelli had been her child's favorite topic since Wednesday afternoon.

A coy grin curved Nikki's lips. "I think he's kinda cute. Don't you think so too? He likes you."

Susan could think of several adjectives she'd use to describe Matt, but cute wasn't one of them. She vividly recalled his sexy-as-all-get-out smile. Irresistible. Now, that was a more fitting description. He'd certainly left an indelible imprint on her mind, and it disconcerted her more than she wanted to admit. "I know what you're up to, Nik, so quit pushing. I hardly know the man."

"I'm not pushing," Nikki protested as they entered the restaurant.

"Yes, you are. I can feel your grubby paw prints all over my back."

"Well, he does like you. I'm not a dumb little kid, you know. I'm in double digits now, almost a teenager. He *does* like you. I could tell by the way he watched you in the hall. So there."

"Barbara Nicole, I don't want to hear another word about that man. He's not my type." Unfortunately, she added silently.

"But, Mom, he *owns* a video store!" Nikki's face lit

up as if she'd glimpsed heaven itself and found it made of chocolate ice cream.

Susan sighed. "You'd think Jack the Ripper was a great guy if he owned a video store. Change the subject, kiddo."

She ignored the mutiny on her child's face and scanned the dining room. The restaurant was packing them in as usual on a Friday night. The sight pleased her. Anna Ling, the owner and one of Susan's first clients, had managed to combine the romantic ambience with good, moderately priced food and excellent service. How far she and Anna had come, she thought proudly, since they'd both begun their businesses on a wing and a prayer.

A hostess clad in a Chinese dress strolled by. "Hello, Miss Dellie, Mrs. Wright. We'll have a table for you in a few minutes."

"Thank you, Amanda. How's school?" Susan asked the college student.

Taking advantage of her mother's distraction, Nikki whispered to her aunt, "Who's Jack the Ripper?"

"A thoroughly nasty person who lived in London over a hundred years ago," Dellie answered, nodding to an acquaintance seated at a nearby table.

"Mr. Martinelli isn't *that* old. He's not British. He's—"

"Nikki."

Startled, the little girl glanced up and found her mother glaring at her. "He's Italian," she finished with faint rebellion.

Susan picked up Nikki's French braid and gave it a gentle tug. "Quit being a pain or I'll feed you spinach for dinner until you're thirty."

"Italian?" Dellie stopped perusing the restaurant for friends. "You didn't mention he was Italian. I knew an Italian man once. Perfectly charming. Met him when I visited my cousin Elizabeth in Baltimore. She's dead, you know. So sad. It was the summer of 1938—when I visited her, not when she died. I'll always remember every moment of those two wonder-ful weeks." Her dreamy expression cleared for a moment. "Or was it three? Mama let me take the train to Baltimore. I was so excited. Twenty-one years old and making my first trip alone. My, but I felt quite fancy-free!" She laughed in a girlish manner, then whispered to Susan, "If your Mr. Martinelli is half as delightful as Carmello, I'd love to meet him."

"Please, don't tell Nikki that," Susan whispered back. "It'll only encourage her."

Dellie gave her niece a puzzled look. "Very well, dear. If you don't want the child to know about Baltimore, she won't hear it from me. Although I can't understand your reasoning. Baltimore is a very nice city. A bit muggy in the summer, but nice. Oh, look. There's Rachel Henderson. Haven't seen her since her surgery. Hellooo, Rachel!"

Philadelphia Simpson's brand of logic strongly re-minded Susan of the ditzy blond comedienne Gracie Allen. Accustomed to dealing with her aunt's non sequitur train of thought, she didn't bother to correct Dellie's mistaken impression.

Nikki suddenly squealed with pure delight. Susan turned to find the girl waving with wild enthusiasm.

"It's him!" The blond braid slapped against Nikki's back as she hopped from one foot to the other. "It's him! See? Over there! Hi, Mr. Martinelli!"

Susan, Dellie, and everyone lined up behind them watched the little girl race toward the man rising from a table partially hidden by a large screen.

"Nicole!" Susan tried halfheartedly to call her back.

Matt greeted the dancing imp with an equally enthusiastic smile. "Hi. I'm glad you're here. I'm getting waterlogged drinking pots of tea all by my-self."

Nikki laughed. "I told you we eat here every Friday night. Did you save us a place?"

"You bet," he said, adding a conspirator's wink.

He looked up then, and smiled across the room at Susan.

"Oh, my," Dellie breathed. "He certainly is . . . *Italian*. I think he favors Al Pacino. I've always wanted to speak Italian. Such a lyrical language."

Susan sighed as Matt's gaze drifted over her jade shirtdress and down her nylon-clad legs to her sling-back heels. She felt a hive coming on. If she had this reaction every time they met, she'd do well to buy stock in Benadryl.

Dellie patted a silver curl into place and stepped toward the man and child.

Susan quickly latched onto her aunt's elbow. "A table will be available soon. Perhaps—"

"I want to speak to that nice young man. Amanda will know where to find us, dear. Come along. We mustn't be rude to your new friend."

Susan wanted to protest that Matt Martinelli was not her new friend, but judging the steel underriding her aunt's magnolia-sweet tone, she realized it would do no good.

She withdrew her hand and glanced around the dining room in hopes of spying an empty table. *Choke down your fortune cookie and move it, buster,* she silently urged a patron who didn't seem in any rush to leave. Seeing no immediate help in that direction, she said to Dellie, "Okay. We'll just say hello, grab Nikki, and—"

"Honey, ye're wastin' yer breath," an elderly gentleman behind her boomed out. "The old lady's within handshakin' distance." He adjusted his hearing aid with stubby fingers. "Shot off the minute you turned your head." He chuckled. "Sprightly, ain't she?"

Heart sinking down into her shoes, Susan looked across the room.

Dellie was introducing herself to Matt. He towered over the five-foot, one-hundred-pound woman. As he took Dellie's hand, his eyes sought Susan's over Dellie's glorious cap of curls. He tilted his head in a pantomime of humorous inquiry and beckoned to her.

Feeling trapped and yet drawn by his roguish smile, Susan gave in to the inescapable social amity and walked forward.

"I'm glad to see you again, Susan," he said when she reached his table.

"Good evening," she responded, cool yet polite.

Mischief gleaming in his eyes, he turned to address Dellie. "You must be the great-aunt Susan mentioned." The mere hint of a devilish grin teased his mouth. "This must be my lucky day, meeting three of the most beautiful ladies this side of the Mason-Dixon."

Flushing a brighter pink than her cotton-candy-pink suit, Dellie warmed to him instantly. "What a lovely thing to say, Mr. Martinelli," she practically cooed.

"Please call me Matt."

Susan almost choked as she recognized the line she'd sworn two days ago her aunt wouldn't fall for. Not only had Dellie fallen for his nonsense, which he had stated with great sincerity and respect, she'd had her socks charmed off. How on God's green earth, Susan wondered, had her guileless aunt managed not to run off with the first handsome, fast-talking traveling salesman to cross her path when she was a girl? As much as Philadelphia Simpson adored a charming man, her choosing to remain single all her seventy-two years was a mystery Susan couldn't begin to unravel.

"Miss Simpson," Matt said, "I hate to eat alone. If I wouldn't be intruding, would you ladies join me for dinner?"

Nikki immediately begged consent. Before Susan could decline, Dellie beamed and said, "We'd be delighted to dine with you, young man."

In the space of a heartbeat, Susan found herself hustled around the screen, seated at his table, and, at his insistence, well on her way to first-name basis. Feeling a bit off center, she agreed to a glass of plum wine when the waitress came around.

Picking up a red and gold embossed menu, she studied the list of entrees and calculated how fast they could get away without being blatantly rude, all the while keeping one ear on the conversation.

". . . raised in Chicago," Matt was saying. "Lived there all my life until two months ago, when I moved here."

Dellie began telling him about one of her relatives, now deceased, who used to live in Chicago.

Susan glanced over the top of her menu to gauge his reaction to the involved and convoluted tale, which had taken an immediate off-track to the wonders of Marshall Field's department store at Christmas, circa 1942. To his credit, Matt appeared relaxed and genuinely interested in her aunt's conversation. People unacquainted with Dellie sometimes found her roundabout rambles disconcerting. Susan mentally shook her head. He was hotter than a southern night and nice as well. A dangerous combination, in her opinion.

Taking advantage of his preoccupation with her aunt, she eyed his clothing. No funky T-shirt and jeans tonight. He was casually dressed in a red sport shirt—red was certainly his color—and navy slacks. She hadn't noticed his footwear before she sat down, and had to resist the inclination to raise the tablecloth for a peek.

". . . and the poodle fell down two flights of an open elevator shaft. Isn't that sad?" Dellie sighed. "It happened while dear Maudie and I were playing bridge in the lobby of the grandest old hotel in Chicago with a couple of the sweetest professional baseball players."

Susan wondered how they'd gone from Christmas decorations in Marshall Field's windows to poodles and baseball players. Matt hadn't so much as raised an eyebrow over the switch, while she felt like she needed a roadmap. Could it be a case of like calling to like? Ditzy to ditzy? She felt a smile tugging at the corners of her mouth, and she stopped it cold.

She'd do well to spend as little time as possible in his company. He was an outrageous flirt with sensual eyes and a smile that set her pulse racing double time. Maybe she was overreacting, but he was the kind of man experience had taught her to keep at a safe distance.

All too often, she reminded herself, beneath a captivating male exterior lurked a selfish, irresponsible boy. She'd been drawn to that kind of man once and had foolishly married him. The only good thing to come out of the relationship was Nikki. Her life was steadily on course now, and she wanted it to remain that way.

Fortified by her pep talk, Susan decided on Szechwan beef with snow peas and laid the menu aside.

"Do you like Italian?" Matt asked her.

She looked at him in confusion. Italian what? she wondered. *Men?*

He grinned as if reading her mind. "Do you like Italian food?"

"I like lasagna."

"If you think lasagna is all there is to Italian food, are you in for a treat. Some night I'll prepare my mother's veal tortellini for you." He kissed his fingers. "It's outstanding."

Susan smiled noncommittally. The chances of his finding a grocery store in the county that stocked anything as fancy as tortellini were slim to none.

"Is your mother living?" Dellie asked.

Let the grilling begin, Susan thought. She knew there wasn't a soul in Millers Creek better at it than her aunt. If Dellie didn't have his whole life history out of him before dessert, she'd eat the gilded plaster dragon guarding the restaurant's entrance.

"No, she isn't," he answered. "Have you decided on what you're having or shall I order for you?"

Awarding him a point for his neat sidestep, Susan waited for her aunt's next line of attack.

"I'll have sweet and sour shrimp. You must miss her very much. It's always so difficult to lose a parent. When did she die?"

"A long time ago."

"Were you very young?"

The waitress appeared with their wine, and Susan laughed silently at Matt's look of relief . The next few minutes were spent placing orders and persuading Nikki to hold it down to one egg roll to go with her standard fare of hamburger and fries.

As soon as the waitress moved away, Dellie asked again, "Were you very young when your mother died?" Her train of thought often derailed in mid-sentence, but Susan knew Dellie was capable of amazing persistence when tracking down information.

Matt filled Susan's glass with wine. "I've been on my own since I was eighteen."

Sympathy fairly oozed from Dellie, but that did not deter her from her course. "You poor dear. So young to be alone. Do you have sisters or brothers?"

Matt reached for his glass of ice water and took a sip. "I have a sister," he said diffidently. He rarely shared personal information with anyone. It was an old habit, born of a maturity forced upon him too soon and the desperate necessity of keeping strangers at bay.

The expectation in the three pairs of blue-gray eyes trained on him made him feel slightly ill at ease. A year before he could have steered the conversation in another direction without effort. But he'd been a different person then. A year earlier he'd been forced to take a hard look at who he was and the way he lived. He hadn't liked what he'd seen.

Susan picked up on his discomfort and smiled sympathetically. "We're prying. I'm sorry."

"No, you're not. Don't be sorry. I don't mind talking to you." And to his amazement, he found it was true. "I just haven't had much practice in talking about myself." Holding on to his water glass as if it might leap from his hand, he wondered what to choose from the thoughts suddenly jumping around in his head. Self-disclosure was more difficult than it seemed.

"My sister Cara," he said slowly, "was twelve when our mother died. All Mother's relatives are still in Italy. My father . . . Well, there was no one else. A social worker wanted to place Cara in a foster home. I'm not sure how I did it, but I talked her into letting me take care of my sister. There were times I wasn't sure we'd make it."

Bittersweet memories floated like dust particles before his mind's eye . . .

. . . A biting wind blew snow across his face as he helped his sister climb down the fire escape of their fourth-floor dump, praying the landlord wouldn't see them and demand overdue rent.

. . . working two jobs, washing dishes in the evenings at the Greek dive across the street for half pay and dinner for two.

. . . a mural of earth and sky Cara painted on his bedroom wall, her attempt to bring color and beauty where there was none.

. . . saving every nickel to buy Cara a prom dress.

. . . drying tears and calming his sister's adolescent fears when he wanted to rest his head on someone else's shoulder and cry.

Matt carefully set his glass on the table. "Cara's married now and lives in San Francisco. She's a graphic artist. I'm very proud of her."

His revelations touched Susan in a way she wished they hadn't. It wasn't what he'd said, but how he'd said it and the things she sensed he'd left unspoken.

For a brief second she'd thought she'd seen a bleak
expression in his dark eyes. She had wanted to reach
out a comforting hand to him, and the feeling disturbed her. She'd rather think of him as a teasing
flirt in red and aqua sneakers and cool Ray-Bans.
Somehow, it made him much easier to deal with.

The waitress returned with egg rolls and soup.
Nikki began telling Matt about all the treasures
stored in their attic at home. "It's filled with the most
fabulous stuff. Fancy old clothes with feathers and
beads, Great-Grandpa's toys, and a wind-up Vic—
What do you call it?" She looked to her aunt for help.

"Victrola."

"Right. There's records and everything. It still works.
Maybe you could come over sometime and we could
play them. You can bring your dog if you want to."

Matt smiled at her. "I'd like that very much. But I
can't bring my dog. I don't have one."

"Oh." Disappointment drooped the corners of her
mouth. "I don't have one either. But if you ever get a
puppy, you could bring it to my house and I'd walk it
and play with it for you."

Hard-pressed not to smile at the hope shining in
the child's eyes, he murmured a thank-you and a
promise to keep her offer in mind.

Susan glared at her daughter. "Nicole, don't pester
the man about dogs. He doesn't want one. *I* don't
want one. Ergo, emotional blackmail will not get *you*
one either."

Nikki glared right back. "I was only being polite,
Mom." She picked up her egg roll and bit the end off.
Mouth full, she muttered into her chest, "Don't see
why I can't have a puppy."

"I heard that," her mother warned.

Hoping to avert the impending war over an obviously hot issue between the two, Matt captured
Susan's attention by passing her the communal bowl
of fried noodles. "Did you grow up in Millers Creek?"

"I was raised here. Moved to Atlanta when I married." She started to leave it at that, then decided there was no reason he shouldn't know what everybody else in town knew. "Nikki and I came back here five years ago after Brian and I were divorced. We moved in with my aunt." Her eyes locked with his. "I can't imagine living anywhere else now. The living arrangement suits all three of us."

Though she'd spoken matter-of-factly, her face revealing no nuances, Matt read the subtle message in the slight lift of her chin. He realized he'd been told that she was quite happy with her life as it was, and he could take the next slow boat back to the Windy City. No one survived the streets of Chicago without developing a skin tougher than a rhinoceros's, though. He hoped it didn't take Susan Wright long to understand that rejection, delicately insinuated or not, didn't bother him at all.

"You've got to see Matt's store, Mom," Nikki said, jumping into the pause. "It's so cool. He has a real theater-type popcorn machine. Customers get a *free* bag of popcorn with every movie! Could we stop by there after dinner? I want to see *Baby Boom* again. Please, please!"

"Not tonight," Susan said. "Besides, you've seen that movie a million times. Aren't you tired of it yet?"

"No. The baby is so cute. I love babies." She looked at Matt. "Do you have any children?"

His eyes twinkled. "I've never been married."

"Oh." Nikki considered his answer for a moment, then repeated, "But do you have any children?"

"Nicole!" Susan flushed to the roots of her blond hair. "He told you he's never been married."

"Oh, Mom. You told me the facts of life when I was six. I know a person doesn't have to be married to have a baby."

Susan wondered if anyone had ever died of embarrassment, or would she be the first? Matt and Dellie looked as if they could fall on the floor laughing. "You were never six," she told her daughter. "You were born thirty."

Matt assured Nikki he didn't have any children.

During the rest of the meal, Dellie pointed out various diners to Matt, explaining who was who and did what in town. By the time they finished the meal, Susan also knew—via her aunt's instincts for getting the scoop—that Matt rented a small house not far from their neighborhood. He enjoyed cooking. His confession that he was a lapsed Catholic prompted Dellie's immediate invitation for him to visit their Presbyterian church. Matt and Nikki agreed popcorn should be dripping with butter. He ran five miles a day. His birthday was August eighth and he was on the down side of thirty-nine. He and Dellie compared notes on books currently on the best seller list, though he admitted he enjoyed spy and horror novels most.

Thanks to No-Subject-Is-Sacred Dellie and Matt's constant prompting, by the end of the meal he was better acquainted with their daily lives than their minister. He knew Susan had eloped at eighteen and that after returning to Millers Creek, she'd worked part-time at the local YMCA while finishing her degree in accounting. Her office was located in their home and her family thought she worked much too hard. Her favorite color was blue.

Susan hadn't been able to prevent her aunt from giving him a complete rundown on their weekly schedule: garden club for Dellie, aerobics class for Susan and herself three times a week, piano and dance lessons for Nikki.

Nikki's contribution consisted of a story about her mom eating a worm on a dare when she was six. Nikki's best friend in the whole world was Billie Jo Brown, who had a VCR in her bedroom and was the proud owner of a dog named Ralph.

As soon as the waitress cleared the table and coffee was ordered, Dellie grabbed Nikki's hand. "Please excuse us. We want to say hello to Rachel Henderson. She had her gall bladder removed last month."

Nikki resisted. "I don't want to. I don't like her. She looks like a toad in that green dress and she always pinches my cheeks. I hate that."

Susan knew perfectly well her sneaky aunt was trying to leave her alone with Matt. "Nikki can wait here with us while you visit."

Once again Dellie showed her steel. "No, she's coming with me. Rachel thinks the world of Nikki. A little visit from her is just what poor Rachel needs." With that she quick-marched the protesting little girl away, saying, "If you don't want your cheeks pinched, keep them out of her reach."

Matt watched Susan staring after them. She looked mortified and as nervous as a teenager at her first boy-girl party when the lights had suddenly been turned off. Adding the few things Nikki had told him about her father to Dellie's insinuations that her great-niece was too wrapped up in her work, he guessed that Susan Wright didn't often relax and just enjoy life. He knew where the road led and it bothered him. She was a beautiful woman who deserved more.

And it was unaccountably important to him that she get what she deserved. What Susan Wright needed, he decided, was the luxury of being romanced.

Three

Matt cleared his throat. Susan's gaze swung back to him. "It seems," he said with a straight face, "I've been thrown to the wolfette. Are you going to try anything? Like maybe holding my hand? Rubbing a leg up against mine? This is a small town. People will talk. I have my sterling reputation to protect, you know."

She gave him a slight smile as her tension began ebbing away. "Your virtue is safe with me. But people are going to talk anyway. Dear Rachel is known as the Mouth of the South for good reason. By this time tomorrow, every one of her acquaintance will know Susan Wright had dinner with her *new friend*, as my aunt calls you. They'll know what we wore, ate, and said."

One of those outstanding, sexy-as-all-get-out grins crossed his face. "I can't think of anything I'd like better than to be called your new friend."

Staring at him, she felt a flutter start in her stomach, shiver over her breasts, and end in rose-tinged cheeks. A woman could get lost in the depths of his eyes, she thought, unable to break the intimacy of the contact.

Neither of them moved for a moment. All background noises, the clatter of silver against china, the murmur of voices, the soft piped-in-music, receded. Heat pulsed through Matt's body. He wanted to reach out, to touch her. Yet through the red haze of desire swimming between them, he knew this was not the time or place.

"May I ask you a hypothetical question?" He was pleased he sounded more together than he felt.

Susan awoke from her dreamlike state and nodded. What was it about this particular man that dissolved bone, muscle, and tissue into a substance no firmer than marshmallow cream? she wondered.

"Suppose," he began, "this hypothetical man met this woman who intrigues him. He realizes something very special could happen between them. Do you think she would agree to give this relationship a chance to develop? I mean, if she wasn't involved with anyone, do you think she'd consent to date this man?"

Date? The Jaguar man? *Relationship?* The words jackknifed through Susan's mind, and her Szechwan beef rose in her throat. Their waitress returning with cups and a pot of coffee, gave her an opportunity to recover from the curve he'd thrown her teetering sense of security.

The simple concept of dating hadn't made her nauseated in years. Since her divorce, she'd dated occasionally. Nice men. Safe men. A banker, an attorney, a dentist, all friends from her childhood and all, like her, too immersed in their careers to demand an emotional investment. They were interested only in an evening of pleasant companionship, and with them she easily maintained a certain detachment. No chance of becoming caught up in something she couldn't control. No chance of being hurt. No risk of anything ending badly, leaving her feeling raw on the outside, and empty on the inside.

She stirred a sugar substitute and cream into her coffee. Matt Martinelli didn't fit her profile for the sort of man she could casually date. In him she sensed an exciting intensity of passion and sensuality simmering just below the surface. Such a man didn't belong in the secure world she'd created for herself and Nikki. There was nothing hypothetical about the way his smile affected her. Merely shaking his hand kicked her libido into overdrive. She couldn't find any safety in the way he looked at her.

The Jaguar man was a risk she wasn't willing to take. Dull but safe would do nicely for her, thank you very much.

Matt eyed Susan with a worried frown. She seemed upset. What kind of man had her ex-husband been that the mere mention of dating threw her into a deadly silence?

He leaned back, took a deep breath, then gently reminded her of his presence. "The women I ask out don't usually panic. They just say yes or laugh themselves silly."

Susan appreciated his ploy to put her at ease. She took a sip of coffee, then met his eyes. "Look, I'm sure you're a nice person."

"My mother always claimed I have some good qualities," he said tongue-in-cheek.

A smile sprang to her lips. "Mothers have to say that. It's part of the job description."

"Why don't you like me, Susan?"

His straightforward question took her aback. "I— I—ah . . ." she stammered. As much as she wanted to be able to tell him she'd hated his sexy guts on sight, she couldn't. Dammit. The man was too attractive. Too incredibly . . . For lack of a better description, she tacked on *Italian*. And she was finding him very likable. But her instinct for self-preservation was deeply ingrained, and she stuck to a polite disavowal. "I don't know you well enough to dislike you."

"That's right. You don't."

Once again her cheeks flooded with color.

"Spend some time with me," he said. "Get to know me. Let me show you how good things could be for us. Will you give me a chance to do that?" His smile touched her like sunshine after a long, dark winter.

"No." It shocked Susan to hear the lack of conviction in her voice. She tried again with a little shake of her head. "No." It still came out wrong, somewhat bemused, clouded by conflicting emotions. She couldn't lower her eyes from his.

Time lost definition. Breath rushed out of her lungs. An odd thought that she'd lost something and didn't know what it was suddenly occurred to her.

Matt watched the confusion spread across her face. He knew she'd meant to cut him off at the knees with a blunt refusal, but it had come out wrong. It was all he could do to hold back a big, pleased grin.

Rising early after a restless sleep disturbed by dreams of deep-set brown eyes and a sexy smile, Susan firmly ejected Matt from her mind. She dressed casually in beige cotton slacks and a blue oxford shirt, sleeves rolled up to her elbows.

Her family was already seated at the oak pedestal table in the kitchen when she went downstairs.

Dellie, decked out in fashion-plate style, was spreading homemade jam on a biscuit. She murmured comments and an occasional "oh, my" as she perused the previous day's edition of the local newspaper.

Nikki was plugged into a bright red Walkman, her small body twitching to the beat. Susan grinned as she listened to her wail out a chorus of "Oh yeah-yeah-yeah, ooooh ye-aah," along with the reigning teen queen of the top forty. Honey dripped from the spoon Nikki held at shoulder level, dropping onto a biscuit lying split open on a plate.

Susan spied a pair of purloined jade earrings in the child's pierced ears. After pouring herself a cup of coffee, she walked over to the table and switched off the Walkman as she sat down.

"Hey!" Nikki yelped. "That was a stinky thing to do. That was my favorite song."

"It was pretty stinky of you to take my earrings without permission too." She held out her hand.

"They match my girl scout uniform," Nikki mumbled as she reluctantly removed them and dropped them into her mother's palm. "I didn't think you'd mind."

"I mind," Susan told her. "Do you have money for dues and your permission slip for the all-day camp next month?"

Nikki nodded. "I'm going home with Billie Jo after the meeting. We're going to ride her horses. Can I have a horse?"

"No." Susan took a sip of coffee, then snagged a section of Saturday's Winston-Salem newspaper lying untouched on the table.

"Not fair. Everybody has a pet except me. I'm deprived. Don't even have a lousy goldfish. You killed 'em."

Susan had the grace to blush. "All I did was change their water, and the next thing I know they're belly-up. How was I supposed to know the water had to sit out overnight? Would you finish your breakfast, please?"

"I'm finished. Don't forget you and Dellie promised to help at day camp."

Susan groaned. "Did I agree to that?"

"Yes, you did. You promised. You're assigned to cooking over an open fire."

"You must have caught me in a weak moment. I can't believe I said I'd do it. I hate camping."

"Wouldn't it be wonderful to live on the moon?" Dellie said suddenly. Her eyes sparkled with excitement, as if she'd already purchased a ticket for the trip.

"What?" her nieces chorused. Nikki giggled, hooked her mother's pinky finger, and said, "Jinx."

"The moon," Dellie repeated dreamily. "I think it would be exhilarating to live on the moon." A frown wrinkled her brow. "Mary Jane," she continued, naming one of her close friends, "says it's all nonsense." She shook her head as if the thought pained her. "Of course, Mary Jane didn't think a man would ever walk on the moon either. Shows what she knows. Mary Jane has no imagination." Dellie turned back to the paper. "Oh, how nice. Rib roasts are on sale this week. Maybe we should invite your young man to dinner."

Susan didn't comment. Her aunt was talking about Matt and she didn't want to encourage the old dear. Matt Martinelli was the last person on earth Susan wanted to share a rib roast with.

Ten minutes later Dellie and Nikki drove off in Dellie's red convertible. Dellie planned to drop Nikki off at her scout meeting, then continue on to Winston-Salem to spend the day shopping with a friend.

Susan cleaned off the table and stacked the dishes in the sink. As she poured herself a second cup of coffee, she mentally planned her work for the day. She was loading the dishwasher when she heard the back door chime.

She opened the door and stared. Half sitting on the porch railing was Matt Martinelli mopping his sweat-dampened face with a red T-shirt. He looked practically naked wearing only a pair of gray jogging shorts, a red and white sweatband, and beat-up running shoes.

"Hi," he puffed out. "This"—he dragged in a breath of air—"is a ro",—wheeze—"mantic house call."

Susan burst out laughing. "Sounds more like you ought to call a paramedic." She laughed again at his disgruntled expression.

"I'm in . . . great shape. Run . . . five miles every day."

She didn't doubt it. In spite of his labored breathing, he looked sleek and sculptured, muscles hard and well-developed. Heavenly days, but he was definitely in great shape. She swallowed back a sigh and reined in her libido. "Well, what do you want?"

"You."

A giddy sense of pleasure sneaked over the walls she'd built around her heart. Something new quivered to life within her. Striving to keep her voice light and teasing, she said, "Cease and desist, Romeo. What do you really want?"

He drew in a large gulp of air. "If I can't have you, may I have a glass of water?"

"I suppose so. Can't have the dead body of a pooped jogger littering my porch. Come on."

"Jeez, Susan." He pushed himself away from the railing. "Don't you have any romance in your soul?"

"Absolutely none," she responded cheerfully. "I'm a pragmatist."

Matt followed her inside, pleased she hadn't turned him away. He hung his shirt on the back of a chair and sat down, all the while watching her fill a glass with ice and water.

"Here, sport," she said. "Drink up."

"Thanks." He glanced around the kitchen as he drank. Decorated in gleaming white and delft blue, it was cozy and efficient. Pots of herbs lined the window ledge. The floor and glass-doored cabinets were oak. He estimated the ceiling at ten feet. Overhead a fan circulated cool air. One wall contained a brick fireplace. Summer or winter, he could visualize a family comfortably gathered here.

Pouring herself more coffee, Susan sneaked peeks at him. She didn't know what to say or how to act with a man who blatantly ignored her brushoff and showed up on her doorstep. Matt was one persistent, incorrigible male.

"I enjoyed being with you last night," he said as she

sat across from him. "You have a wonderful family too."

"My wonderful family thanks you."

"Want to run away with me to Tahiti?"

She couldn't help laughing. His conversation switched tracks as often as Dellie's. No wonder the two of them got along so well. "No. One day in the sun and I'd look like a boiled lobster."

He lifted a heavy black brow. "Picnic in the shade?"

"You always have a comeback, don't you?" She sipped her coffee. "No picnic. No date. No nothing. Look, I'm flattered that you find me attractive, but—"

"Good. That's a start at least."

"—but I'm not interested. I have a busy life. You just don't fit in anywhere. I'm not looking for romance. I don't have time."

He leaned back in the chair, stretched his legs out, crossed his hands over his stomach, and fixed his gaze upon her face. "What do you do for fun?"

Fun? she repeated silently. At the moment she was having trouble thinking about anything but the way the light sprinkling of dark hair on his chest narrowed down to an interesting point that disappeared in sweaty jogging shorts. "I . . . well . . . I enjoy lots of things."

"Name one."

"I spend time with my daughter," she said defensively.

"That's the mother in you." He grinned slowly. "What about the woman? Can't think of anything, can you?"

Valid point, a cynical voice cut through her thoughts. Bubble baths and good books were fun, she insisted. An unwelcome image of herself and the Jaguar man crowded together in a bathtub overflowing with scented bubbles filled her mind. She suddenly felt warm from head to toe. Shaking her head to dispel the erotic scene, she said with exasperation, "Go find yourself a nice woman and leave me alone."

"I don't want a nice woman. I want—"

"One more word on that subject and you're out of here, Mr. Martinelli!" She felt a blush and a hive coming on.

Matt responded with a smile. He loved the way she changed from tough new woman to blushing Victorian maiden within seconds. It made him want to say outrageous things to her just to watch the transformation. "Don't you ever get tired of being alone, angel?"

"No. Do you?"

"Sometimes." He sighed and sat upright, then picked up the glass and drained it. "I used to believe being alone was my preferred life-style. I guess I should go now."

Confusion settled over her as she realized she didn't want him to leave. But it was better that he did because she really didn't want to have anything to do with him. Did she?

Of course not, she told herself as she walked to the door with him.

He turned to her and smiled. "Thanks for the water." He reached out and captured a strand of her hair, rubbing it between his thumb and forefinger.

The simple gesture took her breath away. All she could do was stand there looking into his eyes like an awestruck teenager. He was going to kiss her, she just knew it. And if he did, she suspected she wouldn't have the willpower to refuse.

"Catch you later, angel." Tossing his T-shirt over his shoulder, he walked out the door.

Feeling slightly disappointed, Susan watched him until he disappeared from sight.

Loneliness crept into Susan's office. It was an uneasy feeling, edged with restlessness. She sat at her desk, staring out the window. Tax estimates, misplaced invoices, and depreciation schedules couldn't hold her interest. Matt's question kept running through her mind. *Don't you ever get tired of being alone?*

For the first time in years, she was acutely aware of being alone. She didn't know how long it had been since she'd considered that aspect of her life. Her life was so full with her daughter and great-aunt Dellie. She loved her work and enjoyed its success. She had friends, church, and community activities. With all that, who had a chance to think about being alone?

No, she didn't feel alone. Though sometimes, she admitted, occasionally, maybe, she felt lonely. But it was okay, she told herself. Hell, she'd felt lonely even when she'd been married.

Marriage. What a joke her marriage to Brian had been. He hadn't known how to love someone besides himself, much less known how to be faithful. At eighteen she'd married believing it to be forever. Forever had come a lot sooner than she'd expected.

Why was she thinking about dead history? she asked herself.

A vision of Matt Martinelli floated across her mind's eye. Fatally charming, she acknowledged, from his irresistible smile to his wild red and aqua sneakers. A man like him was capable of making a woman forget her resolve to stay away from such men. It didn't take a Freudian orientation to analyze why her foolish emotions wandered too far in all directions when he was around. He reminded her that she wasn't just someone's mom, not just a businesswoman building her own small empire, not just someone's pleasant companion at a country club dance. Wishing him to Jericho, anywhere but peaceful Millers Creek, she swore to avoid him in the future.

Picking up the Walker's Drugstore account, she lost herself in the constancy of numbers, forgetting the question of being alone and lonely. Unlike husbands and lovers, numbers were consistent. They could be trusted to keep their values. No matter how she looked at one plus one, the answer was always two.

The telephone interrupted her work. She eyed it with mistrust. It could be him. Then again, maybe it wasn't. She ignored the fluttering feeling in her stomach and cautiously answered the call. It was a friend of Dellie's who wanted to know if Susan was dating "that good-looking Italian." She quickly fielded the query.

Two neatly added columns later, the phone rang again. It was Reesa Dunbar, the Billie Jo Brown of Susan's childhood. Reesa said her aunt Rachel had told her she saw Susan having dinner with the man who owned the new video store. After Susan explained the circumstances, she and Reesa chatted about the upcoming spring dance at the country club and promised to get together for dinner the following week.

Another call came in immediately. Rapidly reaching her irritation threshold, she answered with a less than inviting tone.

"Aren't you cheerful this morning," Scott Cantrell, another old friend, said.

"Sorry. I'm working. What's new?"

"That's what I was going to ask you. I heard you're going out with the owner of the new video store. I just wondered if you'd rather go to the dance with him next week. Tell me now so I can line up another date. Reesa isn't going with anyone. I could take her, I guess."

It didn't bother Susan to hear Scott talking about trying to find another date for the dance. She and Scott and Reesa had been inseparable friends for as long as she could remember. She did mind being the topic of the rumor mill, however. "I did not go out with that man," she said impatiently. "We accidentally had dinner together, that's all. Who told you anyway?"

"I had breakfast with Reesa and her aunt this

morning, and according to the Mouth, you two looked pretty cozy last night." Scott chuckled. "Old Rachel said—"

"Scott, since when do you listen to the Mouth of the South? I just met the man, for cripes sake! Unless you'd rather take someone else to the dance, I'll see you Saturday at seven."

After hanging up, she activated the answering machine. In her opinion, men in general—one crazy Italian in particular—were a pain! She went back to work, every ounce of her energy generated by frustrated adrenaline.

She was on a roll when the front doorbell chimed. She groaned and threw down her pencil. Stomping out to the foyer, she was ready to kill the bearer of whatever tidings. She jerked open the door with more muscle than necessary.

Fred Kendall of Kendall's Florist and Nursery stood on the porch. A helium balloon with a face painted on it bobbed behind him. "Morning, Susie." His weather-worn face beamed at her over a dozen red American Beauty roses. "For you," he said, thrusting them into her arms. "Your new beau came in this morning and picked them out special. That boy sure thinks highly of you. Nothing but the best would do. Yes, sir. He's got it real bad."

Susan felt as if her wits had suddenly gone dormant. She didn't know whether to sit down on the floor and laugh hysterically, or scream loud enough to send old Fred running for his truck. The Jaguar man's weird courtship was making her crazy!

A gust of wind moved the balloon forward on its spindly, accordion-pleated legs. The thing nudged Fred in the back as if to remind him of its presence. "Oh, yeah. This here's yours too." He twisted around, grabbed the grinning mylar face, and pushed it toward her. It waved its arms at her, weaving drunkenly on its little shoes.

"Matt thought you might get a kick out of it," Fred

added. "See." He pointed to the balloon person's ruffled paper shirt and bow tie. "It's gussied up like it's steppin' out to the Ritz. All Martha's idea—not giving it to you, I mean—but selling 'em. Folks sure seem crazy about 'em, buying 'em faster than we can keep 'em stocked. Your young man made a powerful impression on my Martha. She said if she was twenty years younger, she'd give you a run for your money." Fred guffawed. "I said, shoot, honey, better make that thirty. You know how the old girl lies about her age. And she said—"

"Fred, Fred." Susan found her voice at last. "I can't accept these things. Take them back. Give Mr. Martinelli a refund. I don't want them."

Fred gently patted her cheek. "You know I can't do that, Susie. Take the flowers, sweetheart. Give Matt a chance. Seems like a real fine young fellow. Martha says he's good husband material for you."

Susan grimaced. She'd just met that pesky man. One accidental dinner and a dozen roses later, and people had them married! That, she decided, was the problem, and sometimes blessing, of living in the small town where she'd grown up. Everybody had an opinion on what was best for her. Well, she fumed, she had a few opinions on the subject herself!

A smile plastered itself on her face. "Just because a man sends me expensive flowers doesn't mean he's the right one for me. I'm not in the market for a husband."

Fred shook his balding head. "Well, you ain't gettin' any younger, and that girl of yours needs a daddy. Almost forgot. Dang, I'm getting too old for this business." He reached into his shirt pocket, pulled out a slip of paper, and read aloud, "'Mr. Martinelli cordially requests the presence of Ms. Susan Wright at dinner at The Red Dragon Sunday evening at seven o'clock. RSVP.'" He peered at her expectantly. "That's French," he prompted, "for letting him know whether you're coming or not."

Susan stared at Fred's hopeful face, then bowed her head over the roses to keep from cracking up. This wasn't happening to her. Things like this just did not happen to *her*! Never had she received a stranger invitation delivered by a more unlikely cupid. She lifted her head. "Thank you for bringing the flowers. They're beautiful. Give Martha my love."

Recognizing a sendoff when he heard one, Fred bade her a good day and made his way down the steps.

Susan pushed the balloon person into the foyer. Just before she closed the door, she noticed a neighbor waving Fred over. It was only a matter of time before half of Millers Creek knew who sent whom a dozen roses. Casting her eyes toward heaven, she whispered, "Why me?"

As she started toward the kitchen to find a vase, a rustling sound caught her attention. She slowly looked over her shoulder and eyed the balloon. It bobbed and weaved on its weird cardboard feet, trailing behind her like a sailor on a three-day binge. Its grinning face seemed to say, Isn't this fun?

"Oh, shut up," she hissed, elbowing it right in the kisser. In response it swayed back and forth, then careened into her backside.

Once again she sighed, "Why me?"

Matt took the bag of popcorn out of the microwave, ripped it open, and watched the steam rise. He inhaled deeply. The tantalizing aroma ranked high on his list of life's little pleasures. It brought back memories of stolen afternoons at the movies when he was a kid.

He remembered slouching down in the faded elegance of the darkened theater, becoming lost in the big screen, and forgetting reality for a while. When he had the money, he'd buy the biggest tub of popcorn available and ask for extra butter.

Giving the refrigerator a look of longing, he shook his head. Those were the days when it had never occurred to him he'd eventually have to dole out doses of cholesterol and saturated fats like pieces of gold from a dwindling pile.

"My willpower knows no limits," he murmured. He upended the bag into a plastic bowl. "I don't need butter. Butter's terrible. Tastes like fish guts."

Unconvinced, he left the kitchen with his butter-less midnight treat before he gave in to temptation.

His rented two-bedroom house was an unremarkable one, standing on the corner of a street in the older section of town, where the homes ranged from brick mansions to tiny frame houses with gingerbread trim. Shady oaks, delicate dogwoods, and some purplish blooming trees his neighbor called crape myrtle provided a screen for blocking out the midday sun. The rooms in his house were small and square, unexceptional but cozy. Matt felt more at home there than he'd ever felt in his high-rise apartment with its spectacular view of Lake Michigan.

In the living room he turned on the television and settled down to munch his way through the late movie. That night's feature was an old romantic comedy, *Father Goose*, starring Cary Grant and Leslie Caron. The actress reminded him a little of Susan, prim and prickly on the outside and warm enough on the inside to singe a man's hands. And classy. Definitely classy. Not sophisticated and elegant with a brittle edge. He'd known his share of such women in his checkered past.

Between mouthfuls of popcorn, he sang the opening song along with Cary Grant. He wished he could have given Susan the roses himself. But not being a fool, he knew it was better at this point simply to remind her that he wasn't going to go away. A smile curved his lips as he thought about Fred's advice. "Susie's going to be a bit stubborn, boy, but don't you give up on her. No, sir, don't you give up." Matt had no intention of giving up. He'd just begun to romance her.

A year ago he wouldn't have dreamed of pursuing a woman the way he intended to chase after this one. Hell, a year ago he might not have given her more than a passing thought. Since meeting her, though, he hadn't stopped to analyze his feelings. He simply accepted them and acted. Funny how he was no longer awed by the radical change in himself. He'd experienced firsthand how precious and unpredictable life could be. When something was right, it was right. "When you find something you want," he said aloud, "you can't dork around, because you never know how long you'll be allowed to keep it."

He'd been waiting for her response to his invitation. So far, she hadn't accepted or rejected it. Several times, he'd almost called her, going so far as dialing the first few digits of her number before hanging up.

"Women are supposed to like roses," he grumbled. Yet Susan had tried to refuse them. Was he going about this romantic stuff in the right way? Romancing a woman wasn't his forte. However, he mused, staring at the television screen, Cary Grant was a pro. Perhaps he'd pick up a few pointers.

Watching the unshaven, unkempt Cary Grant search his one-room tropical-island shack for bottles of booze, Matt frowned. If Susan knew what he'd left behind in Chicago, she'd believe he was no better than the dropout bum the actor portrayed. She was driven by ambition. He knew the look; he'd worn it once. If he wanted to get to know her, he realized he'd best keep the secrets of his former life to himself. Susan would be appalled to know he'd kissed off a lucrative career to open a fledgling video store. Unless he touched her heart, he knew she would not understand.

Sunlight filtered through the stained glass windows, enriching the vivid colors until they shone like polished gems. The church sanctuary buzzed with the steady influx of morning worshipers as they greeted friends and filled their favorite pews.

Dressed in their Sunday best, Susan and Dellie stood at the back. Acting as ushers, they handed out the order-of-worship bulletins along with smiles and words of welcome to the steady stream of people.

"Good morning, Mr. Taylor," Susan hailed a dapper old gentleman. The white rose in his lapel was as much a part of her image of him as his constant cherubic grin. For as long as she could remember, the elderly attorney had worn a white rose in his lapel every day in honor of his deceased mother.

" 'Morning, Susie," he said cheerfully, and handed her two sticks of chewing gum bound together with a rubber band.

She smiled and thanked him. How many generations of the church's children had been weekly recipients of the "Gum Man's" generosity? she wondered.

"Miss Dellie," he said, turning to her aunt, "you're lovely as ever. May I have eight bulletins please. I'll take them along to the nursing home after the service." Politely stepping back, he began to chat with Dellie like the comfortable old friends they were.

Susan, who suspected Mr. Taylor had a secret crush on her aunt, smiled as she watched the two converse. Her admiration for their victory over the encroachment of age swelled along with the Bach prelude being played by the church organist. Mr. Taylor might look older than God, but his vivacious zest for living gave him a youthful radiance.

And Dellie. Susan studied her great-aunt's attractive face, comparing it to the painting of Dellie that hung over the fireplace in the front parlor. She'd been a beautiful woman at twenty. The years since had etched character lines into her face, added a few inches to her waist, and silvered her ash-blond hair. Yet nothing had diminished her vitality and independent spirit. Susan only hoped she aged with such infinite grace.

She heard the footsteps of a latecomer and prepared to hand over another order of worship.

"Good morning, Susan."

She recognized his voice immediately. Slowly she turned to face him. Her heart beat a fraction faster. His honey of a smile flowed over her like a tidal wave. Never would she have imagined he could look so unconsciously elegant in a Ralph Lauren suit. A flush rose to her cheeks, and a hive surfaced on her wrist.

Susan reminded herself she was immune to Matt Martinelli. "What are you doing here?" she blurted out.

Matt resisted a quick comeback to her blatant challenge. So she didn't want him there. He met her cool look with easy composure. "Miss Dellie invited me, remember?" he said. Why did she seem more beautiful each time he saw her? Why did his tie suddenly feel too tight? He had only to look at her to know the answers to both those questions. Susan Wright appeared sleek and untouchable, from her silky blond hair swept back in a classic French twist, to the softly structured dark red dress that fell in graceful pleats from the belted waist. On the surface she looked calm. Yet the expression in her smoky eyes told another story entirely.

Of course she remembered, Susan thought with irritation. Not only had her aunt mapped out their daily agenda for him, she'd practically invited him into their lives. And here he was in beautifully clothed technicolor flesh, giving off an aura of sensuality that even the holy setting couldn't curb her awareness of him.

"I'm sure you'll enjoy the service," she said, striving for a politely distant tone and failing miserably.

"Are you enjoying the roses?" His fingers brushed hers, lingered a moment, then removed the bulletin she'd forgotten she still clutched. The warmth in his eyes wrapped around her like a blanket on a cold and lonely night.

"Roses?" she repeated, sounding bemused even to herself. "Oh, yes. They're lovely. But you shouldn't have sent them."

He simply smiled. "You haven't responded to my invitation yet. Will you have dinner with me tonight?"

She shook her head. "I have other plans." She didn't bother to explain that those plans involved closeting herself in her office with a stack of depreciation schedules.

"Perhaps another time," he said, not seeming at all put off.

"Matt!" Dellie said, smiling with delight. "So glad you could join us this morning."

The organist changed tempo, signaling the entrance of the chancel choir. Nikki and the other acolyte passed by on their way down the aisle. The girl's face lit up when she saw Matt. He gave her a thumbs-up. Her responding grin was brighter than the morning sun shining through the church windows.

"Doesn't she look like an angel?" Dellie said proudly. "But we've no time to stand around chatting now. Come with me, Matt. I'll find you a seat."

Susan watched Dellie lead him away. He glanced back at her over his shoulder. Several people in the row nearest her swiveled their heads around and stared with unabashed interest at the object of Matt's lingering look and cheeky wink. She felt her face flame a brighter red than her dress. The man was incorrigible! Just wait until they saw him sitting with her. She'd be dodging questions right and left after church. When the gossip settled, half the congregation would think her engaged and the other half . . . She didn't want to imagine what the other half would think.

She sighed as she watched Dellie settle him into

their pew. He was as obvious as a lighthouse beacon on a moonless night, plunked down in the pew Susan privately dubbed widows' row. The old ladies would have a field day with this turn of events.

Dellie returned to the back of the sanctuary.

"Why did you do that?" Susan asked her.

"Do what, dear?"

"You know what," Susan whispered a shade louder than she'd intended, earning her a frown or two from people within earshot. "Why did you put him on wid—" She caught her slip of the tongue. "With us?"

Dellie inclined her head in an inquisitive angle. "Where did you want him to sit?"

"In another church."

A beatific smile rested upon Dellie's face. "Don't be grumpy, darling girl. It's Sunday."

Susan dumped the remaining bulletins on a small table. She didn't hear a word of the invocation. Her mind was still reeling. A quote popped into her head, "Mad, bad, and dangerous to know." Lady Caroline Lamb could have been describing Matt Martinelli instead of Lord Byron. Susan prayed she'd make it through the service unscathed.

As Matt settled comfortably in the pew, he looked to his left and met the curious gazes of five pairs of eyes set in sweet grandmotherly faces. He smiled. In unison, they smiled back. The lady seated beside him leaned close and whispered, "Are you Susan's new beau?"

"I'm working on it, ma'am." He held out his hand. "My name is Matt Martinelli."

"Mrs. Boone." She offered him the tips of her white-gloved fingers to shake. "I'm very pleased to meet you. It isn't often we have such a handsome young man share our pew, don't you?" When he nodded, her expression became impish. "Well, isn't that nice. I just may have to get myself a VCR." She turned her attention back to the service.

Silently chuckling, Matt did the same. As he watched Susan perform the rest of her ushering duties, he decided she looked a bit nervous, as though she were constantly aware of his presence. Good, he thought, maybe he was getting to her at last. Something rare and wonderful was happening between them. If he didn't pursue it, he knew she would continue to push it aside. He wasn't angry that she'd first ignored his invitation, then refused it when backed into a corner. She needed time to come to the same conclusion he had. He only hoped for his sake it didn't take her too long.

As she stood straight and dignified with Dellie in front of the pastor, offering plate in her hands, he imagined himself beside her in a very different ceremony. The image was so vivid, it startled him, and he shifted uncomfortably. Wait a minute, he ordered his runaway thoughts, that was going too far. The woman wouldn't even go to dinner with him, for pete's sake! Even so, it was a pleasant fantasy he could live with.

The minister instructed the ushers to collect the offering. As the organ played softly, Matt watched Susan coming closer to him, row by row. When she reached him, she barely glanced at him as she bent slightly to pass the brass plate. Eyes locked on her face, he lifted his hands and deliberately placed them alongside hers. As he drew the gleaming plate toward him, his fingers stroked hers. She let go as if she'd been burned. If he hadn't quickly tightened his hold, he would have had a lap full of money. He chuckled softly. She stared over his head as though fascinated by the stained glass window beyond the pew, then took the plate back and she moved on.

The offering completed, Susan stood beside her aunt in front of the pulpit. She bowed her head while the minister said a prayer of thanksgiving over the collection. Although she'd performed the task countless times without once feeling self-conscious, she now felt awkward. She knew it was because Matt was there, watching every move she made. Dellie had to whisper her name twice before Susan realized the prayer was over. Red-faced, she turned and followed her aunt to widows' row.

Throughout the rest of the service, Susan was keenly aware of Matt. Every time his gaze met hers, she felt the sexual magnetism that made him so dangerous. Her responses went on automatic pilot. Stand up for the "Gloria Patri." Sit down for the choir's anthem. The minister delivered the sermon. She couldn't keep her mind on what he was saying because of Matt's maddening proximity. He was pressed close to her in the crowded pew. They were practically thigh to thigh, hip to hip, shoulder to shoulder. Every time he squirmed provocatively, she was a heartbeat from disgracing herself by trembling from head to toe. At one point he rested his arm behind her on the pew. She almost jumped out of her skin when his hand brushed her shoulder.

During the final hymn she shared a hymnal with him. A crazy emotion stirred inside her barricaded heart. She refused to acknowledge the feeling and refocused her attention on picking out familiar voices as she sang. She recognized Mr. Taylor's rich bass, wavering slightly with age. The sound mingled with Reesa Dunbar's clear soprano. On her right Dellie sang softly, yet expressed everything she felt in each note. Susan felt a faint softening inside herself as she listened to Matt. His singing voice was just like his personality, slightly off key but enthusiastic. She looked up from the hymn book. He was looking at her with an expression of contented pleasure. Her tongue tripped over the words she knew by rote.

Finally, the worship service was over. She experienced a moment of sheer panic. Matt had shown himself to be a man who didn't take no for an answer. He'd ask her out again. She felt her will crumbling like a cookie.

She filed out of the pew behind Dellie. He placed a guiding hand upon the small of her back, and she blushed with sheer delight from the contact.

"It was a beautiful service," he whispered against her hair. "Thank you for inviting me."

"I'm glad you enjoyed it," she said, not looking back at him or allowing herself to think about how right it seemed that he was there with her.

The congregation became a crowd of talking, laughing people. A woman caught Susan's arm and demanded her attention, inquiring about the details of a recent committee meeting she'd missed.

When Susan managed to break away, she saw Dellie had introduced Matt to Reesa. Their dark heads were close together and they were laughing as if they were old friends. She noticed what an attractive couple they made. Somehow she didn't find the idea of them as a couple at all appealing. Pushing aside some very disturbing thoughts, she went in search of her daughter.

Four

He was dressed in black. Black jeans, shirt, and a billowing jacket that looked as if it were made of parachute silk. A red rose was attached to his wide lapel. He looked very much like the Gypsy or pirate she sometimes imagined him to be.

Susan desperately scanned Brownstone Elementary's parking lot. Nikki had just disappeared into the school with the last busload of children. The empty bus rumbled by. Not a soul in sight, except for her in her station wagon. And him.

A quiver of excitement welled up from her stomach. The self-preservationist in her said, *Get this car in gear and hightail it out of here.*

He had seen her too. His lustrous eyes and the million-dollar smile on his urban street face seemed to pin her in place.

She knew she should leave, but she couldn't. Her resolve to forget one mad, bad Italian weakened with every step that brought Matt Martinelli closer.

The way that man filled out a pair of jeans was a crime and a sin, she thought, and swallowed a frustrated groan. Even burdened by a large canvas bag strapped to his shoulder, he walked like unconscious virility on two legs. Just looking at the way he moved brought midnight fantasies to her mind and a blush to her cheeks.

Go! the pragmatist in her ordered. *Are you crazy?* answered the part of her that was totally female.

She felt a bit light-headed when he stopped next to her car. This wasn't happening, she told herself as she rolled down the window.

"Hello," she said. "What are you doing here?" Did she sound as breathless as she felt?

"Good morning, angel." He shrugged the bag off his shoulder and lowered it to the asphalt. "I'm working here today. Videotaping student-teachers."

"Oh, yes. I forgot."

He removed the rose from his jacket, then bent down and rested his arms against the window ledge.

Her gaze was caught by the swirling ruby-red petals as he twirled the flower stem between two fingers. She tilted her head slightly and stared into his mysterious Gypsy eyes. Laugh lines fanned out from the corners. She marveled at the fascination they held for her. Paralyzed by his nearness, she felt her respiration grow shallow. Her gaze lowered to his mouth. What would it feel like to be kissed by that incredibly sensuous mouth?

He traced the rose along the sensitive curve of her jaw. Her spine seemed to melt. Unable to resist, she glanced upward and was trapped by the intensity in his eyes. She felt the faint erotic pressure of the flower petals massaging her parted lips. The words of protest forming in her throat were replaced by her quickening heartbeat.

A quiet settled upon the school yard. Matt felt as if they had been transported into a private world that held only the two of them. The scent of the rose paled in comparison to her fresh smell of honeysuckle and wildflowers. The wistful expression on her face beckoned him. If he leaned just a bit closer, he could taste her lips. He'd thought of nothing else for the past five days. She'd captured his imagination like no other woman. And in his imagination he'd taken her to bed with him every night.

As he lowered his head, Susan instinctively swayed toward him, wanting to be touched, desiring above all else to experience the way this man could make her feel. Her hand found its way to his cheek. It felt warm and rough-smooth against her palm. Confusion welded together with yearning. Her eyes closed against the morning's bright light.

In the pleasure of darkness came the caress of his lips against hers. Cool satin. Searing heat. Desire spiraled along her nerve endings. Her whole body became a conductor for the sensation. He painted a kiss across her lips once, twice. Her response was immediate and natural. The intimate contact deepened, making her feel blissfully alive, affecting her so deeply, it was almost frightening.

Her hand slid down to his shoulder, kneading the silky fabric of his jacket. The feel of his beautifully made fingers slipping into her hair as his mouth hardened on hers was simply glorious. She could swear the Hallelujah Chorus sang through her sensitized body. An emotion so sweet overtook her, she could have wept with joy.

He was unlike any man she'd ever known. In the recesses of her mind, she knew some intangible bond was forming between them. She didn't understand it, nor did she want to. She knew only that it was there, sleeping like a seed in the warm earth, waiting to be nourished to life. She trembled from the strength of that knowledge.

The tardy bell shattered the illusion of their private moment. Reality hit Susan like a fist in a velvet glove, and she jerked away. Emotional shock waves rocked her. Staring straight ahead, she gasped for breath. If she were the wimpy, weeping type, she'd hang her head over the steering wheel and weep her mascara off. She didn't know whether to laugh hysterically or put the car in gear and run over his toes.

"Susan?"

His breath feathered against her face. He massaged his fingers through her hair, then brushed a strand back behind her ear. She felt his hand curve around her nape.

"Don't," she said, trying to keep her voice cool and impersonal. "Don't do that." Steeling herself, she turned a frozen countenance upon him.

He slowly withdrew his hand and studied her face with silent patience. "Don't what?" he asked gently. "Don't touch you? Don't kiss you? Don't want you?"

"All of the above." She shied from the tenderness in his smile. "I don't neck with strangers in school parking lots."

"We haven't been strangers since we met, Susan. I know you. I've dreamed you. And it's appropriate that our first kiss happen here." He tucked the rose in the top buttonhole of her jacket.

For an uncertain moment she looked down at the dark red flower lying against ivory linen. Butterflies quivered in her stomach again. Dangerous. This man was dangerous. It would be so easy for her to give in to what was happening between them. His magic was chipping away at her frozen heart. She didn't want to feel the things he made her feel. With every ounce of willpower she possessed, she denied the emotions he invoked in her.

Forcing her hands to the steering wheel, she held on to it as if it were reality itself. "I told you I don't want to get involved. You are a stranger and I want you to remain one."

"It's too late," he said in a kind tone.

An affirming voice echoed inside her mind. "No." She shook her head. "No, it isn't too late. Move. I have to go to work."

A half-smile flickered across his mouth. "Okay."

He reached for his canvas bag, then stepped back. "You're one hard woman to romance, angel. But I'm not giving up. No matter where you go, I'm going to be your shadow."

Sadness squeezed her soul. "Don't bother. It won't do you any good. Romance happens only in fairy tales. And I don't believe in fairy tales anymore."

Matt watched her drive away. He could swear the scent of her perfume lingered . . . lingered with the hint of sorrow that had laced her parting words.

The following Thursday morning Susan waved good-bye to her plumbing-supply client as she stepped out of his store. Her next appointment was across the street. She walked to the corner and waited for the light to change.

Half a block away, she could see Matt's video store. Although her curiosity was growing stronger, she had yet to set foot in it. Was he there? she wondered. Probably not. He seemed to spend the majority of his time taping at school. And ambushing her.

True to his word, he had spent the last two days being her shadow. She never knew where he might pop up next. He left sentimental greeting cards stuck under the windshield wiper of her car. He whispered outrageous suggestions to her in line at the bank. He joined her aerobics class and royally entertained the ladies with his teasing banter, sexy grin, and muscles all in the right places. She saw him every afternoon when she went to pick up Nikki at school. And he called her every night just to wish her sweet dreams. The Jaguar man was becoming more difficult to resist by the hour and making her a nervous wreck.

The light changed. Lost in thought, Susan started across the street. Halfway to the other side, a car horn almost blasted her out of her beige pumps.

Startled, she stood still and shot an annoyed glare at the rude driver.

Matt grinned his knock-'em-dead grin at her through the windshield of his classic Jag. He lifted his cool Ray-Bans and winked at her.

After several seconds Susan realized her lips were parted and she was staring back as if hypnotized. An outrageous idea leapt into her mind. Matt wouldn't try to kidnap her right off Main Street in Millers Creek, would he? Oddly enough, the notion appealed to her. That in itself was terrifying.

The traffic signal changed again. Another driver impatiently leaned on his horn. Matt kissed his fingers in a parting salute to her.

Embarrassed, Susan fled to the sidewalk. The Jag sped away.

Heath was waiting for her at the door of his shop. The grin on his freckled face told her he'd witnessed the incident in the street.

He held the door open for her. "Susie's got a boyfriend," he chanted.

"Shut up, Heath." Since her dignity was tattered already, she added, "I beat you up in kindergarten and I can still do it."

"That's what you think," he snorted as he followed her to his office in back of the store. "I let you beat me up 'cuz I had a crush on you. Lord knows why. You were just as ornery then as you are now."

"Susan honey!" Myrtle Cooper, the waitress/cook and reigning matriarch of the luncheonette in back of Walker's Drugstore, slammed down a chili dog and fries in front of a customer, then hustled her size-sixteen polyester-clad body around a table to engulf Susan in a hug. "You look pretty as a June bug today. Don't she?" she demanded, slapping another customer on the shoulder. The diner dutifully grinned his approval up at Susan.

"Thanks, Myrtle," Susan said. "How's your grandson?"

"He's a corker, that one. Just put up a Polaroid of the little slugger. Take a peek at the bulletin board before you leave. Now park yourself at your usual table. Mr. Walker's running a bit late today. Said to tell you your young man can keep you company till he can get freed up."

Suspicion arched Susan's brows. Last she'd seen Matt was in the middle of Main Street two hours earlier. He couldn't possibly be lunching here, could he? "What young man?"

"Go on with you! What young man, she says." Myrtle laughed and shook her head. "The one that was sittin' with you in church Sunday. Honey, I was so busy watching him watch you and you watch him during the service that I barely heard a word the preacher said."

"We're just . . ." Susan faltered, not certain how to explain a relationship she herself didn't understand. "Just friends." That sounded reasonable and harmless enough.

A sly grin slashed across Myrtle's face. "Uh-huh. Well, your friend is waiting for you."

"Hey, Myrtle! Where's my fries?" a patron yelled.

"Keep your overalls on, Jake," she shouted back as she headed for the grill behind the counter. "If you think you can cook 'em any faster, get off your butt and do it, you old coot. I only got two hands, you know."

Susan clutched her briefcase tighter with one hand and wiped the sweaty palm of the other down the rough raw silk of her Liz Claiborne dress. The memory of the kiss they'd shared in the school parking lot nagged at her. Just reliving that kiss made her toes curl up.

It simply wasn't fair, she thought as she skirted through the crowd. She didn't want to respond to his smile, didn't want to anticipate these little encounters he engineered. Didn't want to feel that silly suck-in-your-stomach-because-here-he-comes feeling.

He was sitting at one of the chrome and yellow Formica-topped tables, his back to her. She stopped behind him and her gaze locked on the silky black hair spilling over the neck of his red T-shirt, blurted out, "What are you doing here?"

Susan's low bedroom voice wrapped itself around Matt. He set his chipped industrial-grade coffee cup on the table, smiling at the greeting he'd come to expect. Someday he hoped to hear something very different and endearing pass her lips upon seeing him. He turned in his chair to look at her. "Waiting for you," he answered. "Join me for lunch?"

Reading the slogan on his T-shirt, Susan hesitated. Today his shirt proclaimed KISS ME, I'M ITALIAN. On the one hand, she wanted to do just that, and on the other, she wanted to run. It would be in her best interest to walk away. But it was only lunch. And she did have to wait for her client.

Recognizing the indecision written on her expressive face, Matt could imagine the battle of wills she was having with herself. "It's only lunch, angel," he said in a soft, soothing voice. From the widening of her eyes, he knew he'd read her thoughts accurately. His irreverent sense of humor and the wariness in her eyes—were they more blue than gray today?— prompted him to tease her. "I realize you see me as the big city wolf come to foreclose on the farm and gobble you up. But don't worry, even bad city wolves prefer to do their gobbling in private."

Susan realized it would look as if she were afraid of him if she refused his invitation. She placed her briefcase on an empty chair, then settled in the one across from him. "Save the cute remarks, Mr. Martinelli. You don't scare me."

"I'm glad you aren't afraid of me. The last thing I'd want to do is make you feel threatened in any way."

Meeting his gaze, she sat straighter, wearing her

dignity like a crown. "Nobody makes me feel threatened anymore. And don't call me angel."

He picked up an undercurrent in the way she'd tacked on "anymore." For a grim moment a door in his mind that he usually kept locked swung open. An ugly memory came at him from the darkness. The child he'd been raced out and threw himself at his drunken father, catching a raised fist before it could strike his mother. Matt winced, remembering the blinding pain from the blow that had followed.

Susan watched a range of emotions alter Matt's eyes. A teasing light had flickered in their depths, then vanished like a candle flame suddenly extinguished by a gust of wind. She saw anger flare for a second, only to be replaced by something stark and indescribable. Confusion mingled with concern as she placed her hand on top of his tightly curled fist. "Matt, what's wrong?"

"He forced the image back behind the darkness. "Who threatened you in the past?" he asked hollowly.

"What?" She started to withdraw her hand, but he reached out and captured her wrist.

"Who hurt you? Your ex-husband? Father? Who?"

"No one," she gasped in astonishment. "Brian was a two-timing bastard, but he never hit me, if that's what you're getting at. And my father died before I was born. What in the world did I say to make you think such a thing?"

Matt relaxed his grip, rubbing his thumb over the delicate underside of her wrist. "I'm sorry. The thought of someone threatening you, hurting you . . . I overreacted. Please forgive me."

"Of course. But Matt, I—" Susan dismissed the questions forming on the tip of her tongue. His concern for her, no matter how misplaced, touched an emotional chord. The only other person who'd ever looked out for her welfare, besides herself, was Dellie. Still, she felt as if a piece of the puzzle was missing. She wanted to pursue the matter, but it was none of her business. "Shall we order now?"

He nodded and released her wrist.

She declined the creased menu he held out. "I know it by heart. The food hasn't changed in this place since the sixties."

That made him smile. "What changed, then?"

Her answer was delayed by Myrtle's appearance. They both ordered chef salads. "Dellie," Susan continued, "and a bunch of diet-conscious ladies demanded salads. Old Bill—"

"To distinguish him from his son, Young Bill, the pharmacist," Matt added in a tour-guide tone.

Humor lit up her eyes. "Obviously you've met him."

"Oh, yes. He told me all about bass fishing, the sport of *real* men. Even showed me a photograph of his bass boat." She laughed, and Matt liked the husky sound. He wished she'd do it more often. "Sorry I interrupted. Go on."

Susan rested her arms on the table and leaned toward him. "Well, there was another issue besides salads, you see. Dellie was heavy into the civil rights movement. She thought the luncheonette ought to be open to everyone regardless of race or religion. So she spearheaded a petition for civil rights and salads. Old Bill didn't have a single objection to anyone who wanted to eat in his store." She began imitating her client's gruff country-southern accent. "People is people, he said. But he didn't want no *dang* sissy salads on his menu. So Dellie and friends picketed the drugstore for three days. On the third day, Ruth Walker joined the picket line and he caved in. Said it was too goll-danged embarrassing to be picketed by his own wife."

Matt's mercurial eyes sparkled. "Civil rights and salads. Dellie's something, isn't she?"

Myrtle approached their table, laden with dishes and a hearty grin. "You two seem to be gettin' along just fine." She set the chef salads before each of them, then handed Susan a diet cola and Matt a generous slice of apple pie.

He gave the tantalizing pie a longing glance. "I'm sorry, but I didn't order this."

Stern-faced, Myrtle refilled his coffee cup. "You'll eat it and like it. A man can't get by on rabbit food. Needs substance and a little sweetness now and again." She gave Susan a meaningful look, earning a hard stare in return.

Matt grinned appreciation as the waitress walked away with an almost military gait.

"I don't know what fascinates me more," he told Susan as he glanced around. "The odd assortment of clientele, Myrtle, or the place itself. "

Susan poked at her salad with a fork. "What do you mean?"

"Millers Creek reminds me of a Norman Rockwell painting," he said, searching for a way to relate his impressions and the feelings they conveyed. "Stepping into Walker's Drugstore is like time-warping back to the fifties." His gaze drifted to Myrtle deftly flipping hamburgers and trying to avoid collision with two other uniformed waitresses. An affectionate smile touched his mouth. "If Myrtle was seventy pounds heavier, bald, tattooed, and chomped on a cigar, she'd be a twin to a bellowing Greek I worked for when I was a kid. That's what this place reminds me of, Nikos's bar!" He laughed. "Haven't thought about that dive in years." His gaze returned to Susan, and his smile evaporated. If she could breathe fire, he'd be barbecued. "Did I say something wrong?"

She lifted her chin. "Are you making fun of my town? Nobody forced you to come here. This isn't a dive, Mr. Martinelli. It may be a little worn around the edges, but we wouldn't trade it for all the chichi restaurants in Chicago. Walker's luncheonette is a tradition, like our sense of family and community. Something you probably can't understand."

She half rose from her chair, then froze when Matt made a show of quietly applauding her diatribe.

"Why do I have the feeling," he said, "I'm supposed to stand up and sing 'God Bless America'? Don't be so touchy. I wasn't putting anything or anyone down. I love this place. It wasn't my intention to equate it with a dive."

"So what did you mean?" She sat back down.

"Nikos's bar was definitely a sleazy dive." He smiled fondly. "But like this place, it had a charm exclusively its own. It was comfortable—in its way—and familiar, the kind of place where everybody knew everybody else. Nikos owned the bar. He was a rough ex-merchant marine who swore with every other breath, railed at employees and customers alike. But not a soul came in that didn't know he'd lend his last dime if it was needed. He fired me twice a week and shouted bloody murder if I attempted to walk out the door." Matt's intent gaze pierced her. "Thanks to that foul-mouthed Greek," he added in a quiet voice, "my sister and I didn't go hungry."

The picture he painted of friendship and stark reality cut Susan to the heart. She felt like a shrew and tried to smile. "Now I guess I'm the one who should apologize for overreacting."

He smiled ruefully. "You know what I think, angel? I think you deliberately misinterpreted what I said. You're looking for a reason not to like me because I disturb you as much as you do me."

Her startled gaze met his. The accusation was too close to the truth, but like a trooper, she'd deny it for all she was worth. "That's not true."

"Yes, it is. I shake up your routine and you don't like that. You're an ambitious woman. With your business skills you could make a killing in a large city. But you chose to come back here. You've carved out a safe little niche in the old hometown. You want everything to remain the same."

"You don't know what you're talking about."

"I know a lot about you. As you've pointed out, this

is a small town. People tend to talk openly about others they like and respect. From what I hear, I could set my watch by you and tell what day it is without checking the calendar. You've dug yourself a nice rut and heaven help the person who interferes with your schedule or tries to initiate any kind of change. Angel, change is inevitable. Millers Creek will change with the new industry we hope to attract. Nikki will grow up and go her own way in the world. Life does not remain static."

The cold anger on her face as she pushed back her chair and stood up told him he'd zeroed in on an open nerve. "You know nothing about me, Mr. Martinelli. Don't you dare try to analyze me."

He leaned back and surveyed her flushed face. "Who are you running from? Me or yourself? I think you've been lonely too long and you're running scared. I understand how you feel. I've been there."

"Leave me alone. Don't follow me anymore. Don't call me. Don't—just go away."

"No can do, angel. You need me."

She shook her head vehemently. "I don't need you or any man."

"Yes, you do. If nothing else, you need me to keep your life from being overworked and boring."

Susan stiffened. Scarlet stained her cheeks. "I like work. I like boring. I don't like you." She turned and rapidly walked away.

Matt looked after her. It was okay for her to keep running for now. She'd insulated herself so well, he realized, she needed time to come to terms with it. He hadn't planned to shake her up so much, but once he'd started he hadn't been able to stop.

He shook his head as he wondered when she would finally remember she was walking out on her meeting with Old Bill. A chuckle escaped him. He'd bet his video store she'd never walked out on a client in her entire career. When she calmed down, she was going to be some kind of mad.

"I think lunch worked out very well, don't you?" he said to a toddler making faces at him from the next table.

Later that afternoon Matt entered the grocery store, sending a silent thank-you to his very reliable sources—Dellie, Nikki, and Reesa Dunbar. He found Susan in the fresh produce section, examining fruit and vegetables the way he wished she'd examine him. He quietly slipped closer.

For once she wore jeans. He liked how the snug-fitting denim showed off the length of her slim legs and did wonderful things for her nicely rounded derriere. She looked more delicious than the peaches in a soft knit shirt of the same color. Her hair was caught up in a ponytail with a silver barrette, baring the creamy expanse of her neck. He decided if Susan didn't want her neck kissed, she ought to keep it out of his reach. That bit of Philadelphia Simpson—type logic made him grin. Dellie would approve.

He moved in for the kill.

Susan squeaked out a gasp as warm lips caressed her neck. Her body jerked. The produce she held went airborne. A masculine hand stretched out and caught it. She whirled around to face her attacker. The psychic energy of Matt's high-voltage grin sent shock waves coursing through her veins. "Don't fondle my tomato," she sputtered, "you—you Italian Romeo!"

He rolled the tomato between his palms, then set it in the cart. Looking over the items she'd selected, he picked up two oranges. "That's not your usual line." He covered each eye with an orange, imitating a pop-eyed Orphan Annie. "Orange you going to ask me what I'm doing here?"

"I know what you're doing. You're fondling my oranges and making silly puns even Nikki's outgrown. Put them back. I told you to stop following me around. And I'm still mad at you. I missed my appointment with Old Bill Walker because of you."

Matt grinned wickedly and lowered the fruit. "If I can't fondle your oranges, can I—"

"Not another word, Mr. Martinelli."

"Uh-oh. Whenever I offend you sensibilities, you call me Mr. Martinelli. Call me Matt."

"I'd rather call a cop."

"Come on. Say my name."

She sighed. "Don't you ever work?"

"Only when I'm not romancing you, angel. Say my name or —" he glanced at the fruit in his hands—"I'll get down on my knees and follow you all over the store, juggling these priceless three-for-ninety-nine-cents oranges."

She conjured up an image of him doing it. A giggle tickled up from her throat. "Okay, Matt. Stop romancing me and go manage your store."

"My store doesn't need me. You do. Besides, I firmly support the school of management that advocates delegation."

"Oh, really?" She plucked the oranges from his hands. "And what are you going to do when you delegate yourself out of business?"

He tore off a plastic bag from the dispenser and passed it to her. "Devote more time to romancing you, I guess. Are you going to stay mad at me forever?"

"Yes. No. I don't know." Susan turned away, put the oranges in the bag, then dropped them into the cart. She'd thought about him all afternoon, and it wasn't with anger. The man was wearing her down with his perseverance and big Gypsy eyes. "Maybe we could be friends," she said, grabbing for a knot before she reached the end of her rope.

As she looked up at him hopefully, the air became trapped in her lungs, along with all rational thought.

She couldn't remember anyone ever gazing at her in the hungry, possessive way he did, as if he craved sweets and she was the most delicious cookie in the jar. And heaven help her, it was a wonderful feeling.

"I think it's too late for that, angel."

"I hate this damn hearts-and-flowers routine," she whispered more to herself than to him. "I don't trust it. It's no more substantial than air castles and fairy tales. I live in the real world."

He eyed her curiously. "Didn't you read fairy tales to Nikki?"

"No. I didn't want to feed her such nonsense."

He shook he head. "A realist through and through."

"That's why I want you to leave me alone. I am a realist and you aren't. We're out of sync. It wouldn't work out between us."

She pushed the cart down the aisle, stopping to add a head of lettuce to her purchases.

Matt reached around her to pluck a sprig of fresh parsley. "Maybe that's exactly why it would work." He tucked the sprig gently behind her ear as though it were a rare orchid.

His fingertips traced the curve of her earlobe. She fought an overpowering sense of longing. A part of her wished she could believe he was right. But he wasn't. It could never work.

Brushing away his hand, she removed the parsley. "Don't be ridiculous. We'd drive each other crazy inside a week."

"Face it, angel. We have a hot infatuation going and there's nothing either of us can do about it. Want to go to the dinner dance at the country club with me Saturday night?"

"I have a date. Scott Cantrell and I always attend those things together."

Matt assessed her thoughtfully. "He's a lawyer in town, isn't he?" He'd heard about the man in glowing terms from Reesa Dunbar.

She nodded. "A very successful one."

"Is he a practical man too?" The quiet intensity in his eyes seared her.

"Of course."

"Of course," he murmured. "And are you very fond of him?"

Susan laughed self-consciously. For an uneasy moment she imagined Matt could see into the depths of her soul. "We grew up together," she answered, unable to lie under his searching gaze.

Encouraged by her casual description, he smiled. "That's good." A plan to orchestrate the evening to everybody's satisfaction began formulating in his mind. "See you later, angel."

Susan swung lazily on the porch swing on the veranda. Her attempt to absorb the night's peaceful beauty met resistance from an immovable force. The Jaguar man had taken up permanent residence in her mind.

Never had she felt so at odds with herself. Despite her firmest resolve, a part of her was beginning to accept Matt's oddball courtship, was looking forward to bumping into him in unexpected places. She shifted in restless unease. There was no way around it. She liked the outrageous man. When she was with him, she felt alive and desirable. He made her angry. He made her laugh. He confused her unmercifully.

She closed her eyes, absently keeping the swing adrift with one foot while thinking of the things Matt had said to her at lunch the day before. "Change is inevitable." Logically, she knew he was right. But she wasn't sure she was ready for change in the form a half-Gypsy half-pirate Italian wearing red and aqua sneakers.

"Is there room for two?"

For a second she went utterly still. Was there such a thing as "wishcraft"? she wondered. Had she conjured him up with her thoughts? If she were wise, she'd wish him back where he belonged. But wisdom escaped her. For once, she reacted on sheer impulse.

Susan opened her eyes and smiled in the darkness. "There might be. Hello, Matt."

Five

Matt remained in the shadows at the far end of the veranda for a moment, letting a warm feeling of coming home fill his senses. The feeling grew stronger each time he was with Susan. She looked so beautiful sitting on the swing with one long leg tucked beneath her. How could he have considered her face merely pretty the first time they met? Love was the reason. Love made everyone beautiful. Calmly accepting that he was falling in love with Susan Wright, he took the first step toward her.

Susan heard his light footsteps approaching. The swing bounced slightly under his weight. Her heartbeat quickened as he settled close beside her.

"Don't you want to know what I'm doing here?" he asked.

"I know what you're doing here," she answered easily.

"Smart lady. Then you won't mind if I do this." He reached for her hand and laced his fingers with hers.

"Not at all," she murmured, smiling at the now-familiar tingle of awareness from the contact. She savored the perfect fit of her hand within his. His fingers were long and beautifully made, and she could feel their strength in his gentle grip. The human skin, she marveled, came in so many fascinating textures.

"I joined Dellie's garden club today," he said.

Her gaze darted to his face. "You're kidding?"

"Nope. As of this morning I am an official member of the Azalea Garden Club."

Susan heard the pride in his voice, saw how his eyes shone like polished onyx in the night. "Well, congratulations, I guess. You realize you'll be the only person under sixty in the club?"

"I don't mind. Everyone was so friendly. It was like being in a roomful of grandparents, aunts, and uncles. At least, I think it was. My experience with extended family is nil."

She chuckled. "You may find the experience more than you bargained for. That group hasn't accepted anyone new since 1978. Once they do take someone in, they're in for life."

"Really?" He sounded pleased.

"Matt," she said hesitantly, "if you joined as another ploy to get to me . . ."

"I didn't do it for you." He squeezed her hand and gave her a sheepish grin. "I did it for me. When I was growing up, the only greenery in my neighborhood was an occasional weed coming up through a crack in the sidewalk. I've never had so much as a houseplant. It's a good thing, I think, to know how to make flowers and plants grow. Right now my backyard is a jungle. I'd like to clear it out and start over again."

For someone who didn't relish surprises, Susan realized she was constantly surprised by this unpredictable man. He enjoyed children and animals. He was kind to elderly people. He wanted to grow flowers. No matter how outrageously he sometimes behaved, she couldn't deny he possessed some wonderful values. "I think that's lovely. Dellie will teach you how to make a beautiful garden."

The warmth of her smile filled him with serenity mixed with desire. "I promised your aunt I'd teach her to cook Italian. That means I'll be underfoot for a while. I hope you don't object."

"I don't, and if I did, it wouldn't matter. Dellie makes her own decisions."

Their gazes locked. The night air suddenly seemed charged with electricity. Matt wanted to place a kiss on her eyelids, then gradually work down to the bemused smile on her lips. He lowered his gaze, remembering the delectable way her mouth had felt against his. Reluctantly he reined in his thoughts. "I ran across the name Robert Simpson quite a few times during my research," he said, speaking the first thought that came to mind.

For a moment Susan looked at him blankly. She could have sworn he was going to kiss her again. Maybe "wishcraft" didn't exist.

"Was he a relative of yours?" he asked.

She nodded. "He founded the Simpson dynasty. Robert owned the first bank in town and was a real financial genius from what I've been told. He convinced the railroad company to route through Millers Creek, which in turn attracted the textile mills. And of course, he had his fingers in every pie. He built this house. We've been fortunate to keep it in the family."

"It's an impressive house. Built to last. How many rooms does it have?"

The pleasure of having him beside her was making it difficult for her to keep her mind on the conversation. "Do you really want to talk about my house?" she asked curiously.

He released her hand, then slid his arm around her shoulders and drew her closer. "I'm interested in everything about you. And I need distracting."

She waited until her quickened pulse subsided, then asked, "Why?"

He gave her one of his sexy-as-all-get-out grins. "To keep my mind off making love to you."

Her heart fluttered wildly. "You are the most direct

man I've ever met," she said, her voice wavering. Pressure was building inside her just knowing she affected him the same way he affected her. How could she possibly manage small talk knowing he was thinking about making love to her?

"Six rooms," she began, then faltered under his gaze, which was riveted on her face. "On—on—" she stammered, "the first floor." Her mouth went dry with longing. "Second floor, five . . ." Her voice trailed off as his eyes kissed her. Sweet intoxication clouded her ability to form rational thoughts.

His free hand pushed stray tendrils of silky hair behind her ear. "Five what?" He caressed her cheek with the tips of his fingers.

"Bedrooms." The word set her imagination flaring, ignited flames in her mind. Giving up all pretense of interest in the conversation, she tilted her head back over his arm, allowing herself the erotic pleasure of staring into his Gypsy eyes. As though possessing a will of its own, her hand crept up to his face.

Matt rubbed his cheek against her palm. He heard her slight gasp and knew her heartbeat was no steadier than his own. Even in the moonlight he could see her blue-gray eyes were soft with desire. Desire for him. Spellbound with that knowledge, he bent down and teased her tantalizing lower lip with his tongue until she opened to him. Her mouth flowed over his in a kiss that rocked them both with its intensity.

Instinctively, Susan arched her body toward him, winding her arm around his neck. He filled her senses. She burned with need.

Matt felt his willpower disintegrate. Another second and he'd find himself over the edge with wanting and loving this woman. He broke away, groaning a barely audible Italian curse.

Susan sat up straight. Necking on the front porch like a randy teenager, she thought, almost laughing aloud from the absurd joy of the moment. She folded her hands primly in her lap. Biting her kiss-swollen lower lip, she concentrated on regaining her equilibrium.

"Distraction," she heard him mutter in a ragged, breathless voice. "Did you grow up in this house?"

"Yes. Dellie raised me." She relaxed again and laid her head on his shoulder. "My father died before I was born and my mother died when I was four. I have few memories of her. Dellie taught me the social graces, how to play a wicked game of poker, and the secret of making elderberry wine."

His laughter rippled through the air. Smiling in response, she glanced up. Just looking at him brought on a now-familiar heat. Being with this man aroused the most incredible feelings in her. For once, she truly wished she believed in romance, fairy tales, and all things happily-ever-after.

"What was it like growing up in Millers Creek?" he asked.

"Nice. Not exciting, but nice. Reesa Dunbar, Scott Cantrell, and I were best friends from the cradle. We climbed trees, skinned our knees roller skating, got in trouble together, and took the usual lessons together—piano, ballroom dancing, and art. It was Scott who dared me to eat that worm Nikki told you about. Everyone knew us, looked out for us, didn't hesitate to tell our families about our misdeeds or slip us quarters for soft drinks at high school football games. We could never get away with anything. Still can't."

The laughter forming in her throat evaporated. He was looking at her in that hungry way again. A thrill of excitement shivered down her spine.

Matt could not resist giving her a hard, quick kiss. Smiling against her parted lips, he whispered, "Sounds like a nice way to grow up, angel."

Heavenly days, she thought, mentally fanning her overheated face. Kissing Matt was rapidly turning into her favorite pastime. Distraction. She needed a bit of that herself. She cleared her throat.

"What did you do in Chicago? Did you have a video store there?"

Matt sat back slightly. He'd known she'd ask eventually. He was prepared. "No. I sold computers." It was the truth reduced to its lowest common denominator, he told himself in reaction to a flash of guilt.

Susan nodded. A salesman she thought. That made sense. Given his personality and blinding smile, he could no doubt sell ice cubes to Eskimos, heaters in the tropics. "I imagine you were a very good salesman. Why the change in careers? Did you get bored with computers?"

"I still love playing with them. I just didn't want to sell them anymore. It was time for change."

"Do you miss the city?"

"No."

Puzzled by his attitude, she frowned. "How could you not miss it even a little? You grew up there and stayed most of your adult life. Surely, there's something you miss."

"The Field Museum of Natural History, and a hole-in-the-wall restaurant that serves the best pan pizza in the world."

She laughed. "That's it?"

"The Adler Planetarium comes in a close third," he joked, but then the teasing left his eyes. "Once Cara graduated from college, she moved to California. After she left home, it was merely the place I lived." He was silent for a moment, then continued on as though lost in a fond memory. "The museum was my birthday present every year since I can remember. Mama would take the day off from work, and we'd explore the place from top to bottom. After Mama died, I kept up the tradition by taking Cara on her birthday. This will be the first year I've missed it."

Based on his appearance and laid-back-life style, Susan had judged him to be a person who lived for the moment, doing whatever his inner music directed. His revelation proved her wrong. Family and tradition were important to him. She touched his cheek. "Old Salem is only an hour's drive from here. It has a restored Moravian village and MESDA, the Museum of Early Southern Decorative Arts. It's one of my favorite places. I'd love to share it with you."

Covering her hand with his, Matt slid her warm palm to his mouth and pressed a lingering kiss upon it. He hoped her favorite place was only the first of many things she would want to share with him. "Thank you. I'd like that very much."

The sparkle in her eyes faded. She glanced away, then turned back to him with a serious expression. "I've been thinking about what you said to me at lunch. I did come back here because it offered safety. I needed the security of something familiar, something I could count on to remain stable and unchanging. You probably think I'm a coward for running home, but—"

"I understand why you came back, angel." He rubbed the back of his hand across her cheek. "There's no shame in coming home to people who love you. I said those things because I felt you were trying to shut me out without even knowing who I really am. I only wanted a chance to become a part of your world."

He stared into her eyes the color of a warm silvery-blue ocean. "I know you fly with your own wings. That's the way it should be. I just want to soar beside you. If you'll let me."

Suffused with emotion, Susan touched her lips to his. She knew she could make no promises. But she would try to let him into her life just a little.

Early Saturday evening, Susan lounged in her claw-foot bathtub, her head resting on the rim, her eyes closed. The hot water and scented bubbles felt luxurious. She laughed out loud as she thought of the card she'd received in the mail that morning. On it Matt had written: Roses are red. Violets are blue. I've got the hots for you.

Original it wasn't. Matt was no poet. But he was sweet and corny and crazy and—

Fun.

How long had it been since she'd allowed herself simply to have fun with a man? A thousand years and a heartbreak ago. Susan sighed and raised her foot, trying to twist the hot water faucet with her toes. It refused to budge. She sat up, turned it on to a drizzle, then lay down again.

Where had Matt been all day? she wondered. She hadn't run into him anywhere. Somehow his absence made him all the more conspicuous. She couldn't help feeling disappointed. The rat.

He really wasn't her type, she thought, blowing a handful of bubbles into the air. She was used to the conservative oxford-cloth-button-down kind. The kind who was more concerned with tax shelters than romance. Then again, if Matt was her type, a ribbon-wrapped packet of cards and notes wouldn't be hidden in her lingerie drawer.

"Good *eve*-ning, Mother." Nikki stood at the open door with one hand negligently propped against the doorjamb, the other tucked on her outthrust hip.

Susan bit back a grin. Her daughter was dressed in one of her ivory silk and lace slips. A 1940's wide-brimmed hat made of dark green faille was perched on Nikki's golden head, its long, curling black feather trailing to her shoulder. Black slingback heels with rhinestone clips practically swallowed her tiny feet.

"Good evening, my lady. Going somewhere?"

"To the country club dance." Nikki clumped over to the vanity where she picked up a makeup brush, applied blusher to her cheeks, then critically examined herself in the mirror. Her gaze dropped to the lacy bodice gaping over her flat chest. "Billie Jo's getting bosoms. She has a bra. Her mother bought it for her." Nikki liberally smeared her mouth with lipstick. "Billie Jo refused to go to the store to buy one. She was afraid somebody might see her. So Mrs. Brown got one for her." Nikki sighed. "Do you think I'll ever get any?"

Susan turned off the hot water. "Sure. You can wear a bra if you want one."

"I mean bosoms. Do you think I'll ever grow any?"

Susan smiled reassuringly. "You will, I promise. Be patient. It'll happen."

"I know." The child reached for a long strand of pearls lying on the vanity. "I just hate to be left out." She took off the hat, looped the necklace twice around her throat, returned the hat, and posed seductively. "Billie Jo says Matt's a hunk and a half."

"How precocious of her," Susan murmured.

Nikki peeked at her mother out of the corner of her eye. "I think he's charismatic. I looked up the word. It means—"

"I know what it means, Nicole."

"Matt is so interesting. He's been to Japan. Imagine that. All the way to Japan, and Australia too. Koala bears live in Australia. Wouldn't it be neat to have a koala bear as a pet?"

"Uh-huh."

"Matt knows more about computers than the computer lab teacher at school. The principal is letting him teach us how to use video equipment. Isn't that simply fabulous?"

"Fabulous," Susan repeated absently, wondering about the purpose of Matt's trips to such exotic places. Business or pleasure? She rubbed soap on a washcloth. So far, she hadn't delved too deeply into his life before Millers Creek, but curiosity consumed her more each day. She also had a feeling her family knew more about him than they let on.

"Don't you wish you were going to the dance tonight with Matt?" Nikki asked.

Wishing the same thing, Susan spoke more sharply than necessary. "Well, I'm not. Change the subject, kiddo." Who was Matt taking to the dance? she wondered as she lifted her leg to scrub it.

"Why don't you wear other nail polish colors beside pink?" her daughter asked. "Mrs. Brown has lots of different colors. Even sparkly silver."

"Why don't you sparkly-silver yourself out of here and go to bed?"

"It's only five o'clock!" Nikki turned her nose up in the air and clip-clopped out.

Susan sighed. She raised her leg again and stared at the nail polish on her toes. Pink. It was the only color she wore. Had her life become as predictable as the color of her nail polish? Nikki seemed to think so. Matt definitely thought so.

Rising, she stepped out of the tub and reached for an oversize towel. Everything had been perfect—until he came along.

Maybe he'd asked Reesa to the dance. A twinge of jealousy slipped on easier than her robe. She knew she had no right to get all green-eyed over his escorting someone else. After all, Matt had asked her first and she'd turned him down. Dammit.

She'd known him less than two weeks. How could that wonderfully crazy man shake her up in such a short time? It wasn't fair. She didn't want him to make her laugh, or show her how dull her life had become, or make her want something she didn't have.

But he did. And she knew those feelings were not going to go away. "A pox on you, Martinelli," she said, but she couldn't stop a slow smile as she decided she'd take the initiative and ask him to dance with her that night.

Susan descended the stairs, her hand lightly skimming the mahogany banister. She glanced at her freshly polished crimson nails and smiled. Down below, an admiring audience of two waited on the landing. Nikki clapped and whistled loudly. Excitement glowed in Dellie's eyes.

"You're going to be the most beautiful lady at the dance, Mom. Prettier than Miss America. Prettier than—" Nikki paused. "Prettier than Debbie Gibson!"

Susan smiled. "Thank you, baby."

"Oh, my," Dellie breathed, one hand fluttering up to greet her niece. "You look so elegant."

Susan took her outstretched hand and gave it a little squeeze. "The dress is beautiful. Thank you for letting me wear it."

"You're welcome, darling girl. Heaven knows why I saved it all these years. Just couldn't bear to part with it, I suppose. We Simpsons are terrible pack rats. My mama saved the strangest things. Your grandfather and I used to tease her unmercifully." Dellie's face took on a pensive expression. "I wonder if your christening dress is still up there, dear."

"Tell me again about when you wore the dress," Nikki begged her aunt as they all walked into the parlor to wait for Susan's date.

"It was 1924," Delli began. "Or maybe 1923? Anyway, Mama and I went to New York to buy gowns for my cousin Amelia's coming-out ball. We tried on hundreds of dresses and had the loveliest time. Mama bought a tea length gown in the softest shade of rose. When I saw the one your mother was wearing, I fell in love with it! Amelia's ball was held in Raleigh. It was *the* affair of the season. The governor attended. I danced with him. Such a charming man. I felt so beautiful . . ."

Susan wandered aimlessly around the room, barely listening to her aunt. Catching her reflection in a gilt-framed mirror, she stopped and stared. Even though she'd studied her reflection upstairs, she still hardly recognized herself. It was easy to see why Dellie had fallen in love with the dress. It was designed to make a woman feel beautifully feminine. The 1920's slim sheath was made of a clinging dark peach fabric shot with sliver threads. The neckline draped low from thin straps, revealing a hint of cleavage. Beaded fringes hung saucily from the drop waist, decorating the above-the-knee-length skirt.

Bemused by her own appearance, she wondered why she was wasting such a dazzling gown on Scott. No matter what she wore, he invariably said, "Susie, you look real nice." She always mentally added a mock punch to her arm, just as he'd done when they were kids and had been partners for a ballroom dance recital. She laughed quietly at herself. "Might as well have on a pinafore and patent leather Mary Janes," she murmured.

Giving her image a last rueful glance, she turned away. It wasn't that she was vain, she thought, but it would be nice to have a man truly look at her with admiration.

The door chime interrupted her thoughts. "Scott's here," she said. "Come and say hello."

Dellie and Nikki exchanged a peculiar glance. "You go first," they choroused. Flushing a rosy pink, Dellie added, "We wouldn't want to spoil the moment for you. Go on. We'll come along in a minute."

Those two had barely been able to contain their excitement all day, Susan mused, cooing over the dress and wondering how her date would react. Now that he was there, they were hanging back. Shaking her head over their odd behavior, she walked out into the foyer, and opened the door.

The admiration she'd wished for only moments before gleamed at her from Matt's eyes.

Susan simply returned his steady gaze. Her heart hammered so loudly against her chest, she wondered if he could hear it. Unable to voice the questions ricocheting inside her head, she allowed her gaze to travel over him.

He wore an expertly tailored black tuxedo, a crisp

white pleated shirt, and a black tie with natural confidence and careless Bogartlike elegance. The man was splendid, she thought over the deafening pulse in her throat. Unassuming splendor from his footwear—appropriate shoes for the occasion, thank heaven—to the top of his raven's-wing hair. A flush of pleasure rushed over her like fever. A smile trembled on her lips.

Matt felt dazed, as if he'd been hit by a two-by-four. Thousands of silver threads on the incredible creation skimming Susan's body caught and reflected the porch light, giving her the illusion of shimmering. She simply took his breath away, especially when he noticed how well the dress displayed her long legs. He deliberately glanced up and away, realizing that if he didn't breathe soon, he was a dead man.

Returning his gaze to her, he cleared his throat and broke the silence. "There are no words adequate enough to describe how beautiful you look."

Susan found her tongue at last. "What have you done with Scott?" she asked, her voice betraying no more than mild curiosity.

He laughed. It was truth time. At least a truth of some sorts. "Nothing. He's unharmed, I assure you. We're . . . ah, double-dating tonight, you see."

"We are?"

"Ah, yes. We'll meet Scott and Reesa at the country club."

"We will?"

Matt felt his tie constricting like a noose. "Right. We'll meet them there. I volunteered to drive you to the club, since your house is right on the way. My Jag's an XKE. Holds only two people." It was lame. He knew it. He knew she knew it. It was so lame, a crutch wouldn't help. He prayed she wouldn't slam the door in his face.

She smiled. "How very considerate of you."

He could have kissed her in sheer relief.

"Hi, Matt!" Nikki cried gleefully.

He peered around Susan and waved. "Hi, Nik, Miss Dellie. How are you tonight? Long time no see, huh?"

Nikki's head bobbed rapidly up and down. "Right. Haven't seen you in ages. Haven't talked to you either. Right, Dellie?"

Susan's eyes narrowed on her family. They stood just out of her reach, wide grins plastered on their faces. They weren't at all surprised to see Matt. She added their insistent pleas for her to wear this particular dress to their unusual excitement over her date and their all-too-innocent expressions and came up with a conspiracy. A conspiracy that included her two best friends. The darlings! The double-crossing, matchmaking darlings.

Holding her family's gaze, she said, "You knew about this, didn't you?"

Her aunt blinked. "The dinner dance? Certainly, dear. It's an annual event. Lovely music and Japanese lanterns on the terrace. So romantic. When I was a girl, we used to dance until dawn and—"

"Never mind," Susan said with a shake of her head. The two conspirators beamed happily. She decided to look upon this turn of events as a gift, one that she would simply accept and enjoy for the moment.

She smiled at her aunt and daughter. "Good night, loves." Removing a matching beaded jacket and evening bag from a table beside the entrance door, she turned to face Matt. "I'm ready now."

It was a perfect evening for the country club's spring dance. A full moon and a sprinkling of stars lay against the black silky sky. The April night was clear and the air felt crisp and clean. The main dining room glowed with candlelight. Sheer sea-green draperies hung from the glass wall looking out to a pool filled with floating candles. Beyond a series of open French doors, colorful Japanese lanterns softly illuminated the terrace and garden. Inside, people crowded around the buffet tables, admiring the ice sculptures and loading their plates. Others mobbed the two bars set up on either side of the room.

Music floated on the air as lightly as the caressing spring breeze as Matt stepped out onto the terrace with Susan. For a moment they watched the couples dancing to a romantic Paul McCartney ballad played by the live band.

"Dance with me?" he asked in a husky whisper.

Light cast a reflection in his dark eyes, giving Susan a fleeting impression of fire and brandy. An unaccustomed shyness assailed her. All she could do was nod.

Very aware of the man beside her, she allowed Matt to guide her back inside to the dance floor.

Matt gathered her into a light embrace. All week he'd imagined how she might feel in his arms. Now he knew. The touch of her skin, her soft curves molding perfectly to the lean contours of his body, and the way her golden head nestled between his shoulder and neck were better than his imagination. Baby-fine hair and her warm breath feathered his cheek. Tenderness welled up inside him.

Susan felt her heart beating with the rhythm of the music. Their steps were evenly matched, and she easily, mindlessly followed his lead. The gentle massage of his hand on her back and every swaying movement charged the air with sexuality. Sweet emotion for this man filled her heart. For a moment she felt too fragile to contain it. The feeling was too powerful, too fast. It frightened her a little. She shivered under the impact.

"Cold?" he whispered into her hair.

"No." Her hand slid farther across his shoulder, and she turned her face into his neck. His throat was only a kiss away. Desire that had long lain dormant spilled out like water pouring through a broken dam.

The Publisher of Loveswept® Romances invites you to:

CLAIM A FREE EXCLUSIVE ROMANCE

Lift Here

...PLUS SIX ROMANCES RISK FREE

6 ROMANCES RISK FREE

Detach and affix this stamp to the postage-paid reply card and mail at once!

NO OBLIGATION TO BUY!
THE FREE GIFT IS YOURS TO KEEP

SEE DETAILS INSIDE ▶

YOU GET SIX ROMANCES RISK FREE...
Plus AN EXCLUSIVE TITLE FREE!

Loveswept Romances

This FREE gift
is yours to keep.

MY "NO RISK" GUARANTEE

There's no obligation to buy and the free gift is mine to keep. I may preview each subsequent shipment for 15 days. If I don't want it, I simply return the books within 15 days and owe nothing. If I keep them, I will pay just $2.25 per book. I save $3.00 off the retail price for the 6 books (plus postage and handling, and sales tax in NY).

YES! Please send my six Loveswept novels **RISK FREE** along with my **FREE GIFT** described inside the heart! **BR9**   41228

NAME_____

ADDRESS_____APT_____

CITY_____

STATE_____ZIP_____

DETACH AND MAIL CARD TODAY

FREE BOOK OFFER!

She closed her eyes, wanting the music and their dance to go on forever.

The crowd pressed them closer together. Enjoying the feel of his arms tightening around her, Susan almost sighed with pleasure. Intoxicated by all the sensations he engendered in her, she indulged in something she'd wanted to do since the day they'd met. Her fingers slipped into his raven hair. Pure silken heaven! A soft groan escaped him, and she smiled in delight. It was good to know she wasn't the only one deeply affected by moonlight-and-music madness.

She rubbed her cheek against his shoulder and hummed the tune quietly to herself. Lazily opening her eyes, she glanced over to the other dancers and spotted Scott and Reesa. She lifted her hand to wave, but they didn't see her.

They were locked together, barely moving. Scott wore a silly, bemused smile. He was staring at Reesa's upturned face as if suddenly discovering that the skinny, metal-mouthed playmate of his childhood was a lovely woman. Susan realized something had just clicked between her two friends and smiled at them with affection. It seemed right that their caring friendship should develop into something deeper.

The tempo escalated as the band smoothly segued to a livelier piece. Reluctantly, Susan tilted her head back to look into Matt's eyes. He blinked. His bewildered gaze flickered over the other people, who had automatically switched to a vigorous pace.

"What are they doing?" he asked.

"The shag." She laughed at his confused expression. "We claim it as our own addition to beach music. It evolved in the early sixties, I guess. Every band that hopes to get a job in North or South Carolina knows they better have a large repertoire of beach music for us shag-crazy folks."

"Hey, Susie! Let's show these bums how to shag!" A

hulking six-footer dived through the throng and smacked a kiss on top of Susan's head.

All Matt could see was shoulders. Shoulders a player for the Chicago Bears would kill for. His hold on Susan tightened possessively.

"Hello, Heath," she greeted the red-haired giant. "Where's Lynn?"

"Resting her feet. Said her toes were black and blue from my stomping all over 'em. She just can't keep up with the master, that's what I say." Heath eyed the dancing couples bumping into them. "Come on, Susie, let's cut a rug."

Glancing at Matt, Susan recognized the storm gathering in his eyes. "Some other time." She introduced the two men. "Matt, you remember Nikki talking about her best friend Billie Jo Brown. Heath is her father."

Matt smiled politely, accepting the big paw thrust at him.

"Glad to meet you," Heath said, vigorously pumping Matt's hand. "You're the man with the Jag. I'd kill for a car like that. Heard a lot about you. Welcome to Millers Creek. My kids practically live in your video store. Do me a favor and kick 'em out once in a while."

Matt laughed. Although he found it impossible not to like the jovial man, he wished the guy would fade back into the crowd and leave them alone. "Nice to meet you too. Are you the Heath of Heath's Sporting Goods on Main Street?"

Heath grinned proudly. "That's me. Stop by the store for a cup of coffee and I'll tell you about the time Susie beat me up in kindergarten."

Susan flushed. "I did not beat you up. I just gave you a black eye for trying to peek up my skirt."

"Was it worth it?" Matt couldn't resist asking Heath, tongue-in-cheek.

"Don't know. Didn't get a chance to see anything but stars once her fist connected with my face."

"Very funny, boys," Susan said dryly. "Buzz off, Heath."

The man grinned. "Okay. I know when I'm not wanted. Wish Miss Dellie was here. She wouldn't turn down a chance to shag." With that he swam back through the crowd, bellowing, "Does anybody want to dance?"

Susan laughed and shook her head. The mood had been broken and she didn't know quite how to recapture it. Looking at Matt, she saw her disappointment mirrored in his eyes. "Do you want to sit this one out?"

"Sure. Would you like a drink?"

They headed toward the bar, and Matt was content to allow her to lead. In fact, he was delighted to follow in her shimmering wake. Once or twice he caught interested glances sent her way. Apparently, he wasn't the only man in town who thought she had outstanding legs and a great backfield in motion. The idea didn't sit well with him. As far as he was concerned she belonged to him lock, stock, and legs. When those same men looked at him, he warned them off with a no-trespassing glare.

When they reached the bar, Matt took two flutes of champagne from the bartender, then scanned the room for a secluded spot. Every table was taken. People stood in tight groups, laughing and talking. Unless he could persuade Susan to hide with him behind a huge potted plant, privacy wasn't going to be found here. The pool area caught his eye. Not a single soul lingered there.

He bent his head to hers. "It's too crowded and hot in here. Let's walk outside." Without waiting for an answer, he tucked her hand in the crook of his arm and waded through the crush.

They strolled along the azalea-lined stone path to the swimming pool. The faint music mingled with the gentle lap of water against the pool's blue and white tiles. A lover's moon and floating candles provided the only light.

Feeling shy again, Susan withdrew her hand and walked to the edge of the pool. Gazing down at the candles shaped like water lilies, she silently tested various conversational gambits. Small talk held no appeal, though. She was at a loss for words. In fact, she didn't want to talk at all. What she really wanted, she mused wistfully, was to step outside of herself, even if for only a little while. If she had the guts, she'd simply reach out and draw his lips to hers. Dellie had taught her to be a lady. Gently bred women didn't grab men and kiss their socks off. At least, she'd never done so.

What absolute silliness, she thought. She lifted her head as her confidence spiraled upward, then pivoted slowly.

His champagne glass halfway to his mouth, Matt froze. Susan's smile was sensual dynamite. It exploded in his brain. Somewhere in the back of his mind he registered the cool touch of her hand upon his face, her long finely made fingers slipping into his hair, their persuasive pressure urging his head downward. He stared into her eyes, then his own eyes closed and he swam in sensations, as if he'd been dipped into a calm sea.

Susan lightly touched her lips to his, then caressed his mouth with a full-fledged kiss that set off sparks like spinning Catherine wheels on the Fourth of July. Desire curled inside her. It was too much. It wasn't enough. She moved closer to the heat of his body. He wrapped an arm around her waist, drawing her upward, fitting her snugly to him. She focused solely on the feel of his lips parting hers. The sexual tension rose with the invasion of his tongue, and she thought she'd go mad with wanting. The Catherine wheels spun faster. She groaned as they spun completely out of control.

The pounding of Matt's heart took on a tribal beat.

Caught up in the desperate hunger she ignited, he ran his hand along the length of her back. Cupping her firm bottom, he drew her into the cradle of his hips. Every passing second burrowed her deeper into his soul. Never had he wanted so fiercely. He wanted to make love to her, wanted to find some way to release everything she seemed to hold so tightly inside.

Reason finally intruded and demanded he end the exquisite torture. Reluctantly, he raised his head and drew in a ragged breath. She rested her forehead against his chest. Placing a finger under her chin, he tilted her face up to meet his eyes. For a long moment they simply gazed at each other.

Unable to stand the silence, or the undisguised desire in his eyes, Susan glanced away, then back again. She smiled slightly. "I think I'm a bit embarrassed."

"Why?" He stroked her cheek. "Because you poured your wine out on the concrete?"

She followed his twinkling gaze to her empty glass. Laughter bubbled up in her throat. "Parking lots, swings, and swimming pools." She shook her head. "We find some strange places to kiss."

Matt grinned. He debated himself for a second, but couldn't resist the opportunity she'd just handed him. "I'd love to find every one of your strange places and kiss them."

Needing a little distance, Susan walked over to the diving board and sat down, then looked at him. Given the black night and his dark clothing, he could have faded into the shadows. But his rough-cut features were clearly visible in the flickering of the candlelight, and she saw the desire still burning in his eyes. "You are incorrigible," she whispered.

"You are beautiful," he answered, striding toward her.

Her gaze dropped. Why did this man affect her so? she wondered. She'd enjoyed the company of men over the last few years, but never had she imagined allowing any of them into her life, much less her bed.

Until now. Now she could think of nothing else.

She looked up. A ghost of a smile flitted across her lips. "You're a flirt, Romeo." And so much more, she silently added.

He removed the champagne flute from her unresisting fingers and set both glasses beside her. "Not so, Juliet. I'm serious." Leaning down, he brushed a kiss across her mouth. "Very serious. About dancing with you."

She glanced toward the terrace. "They're still playing beach music. Shall I teach you to shag?"

"Teach me anything you want, angel."

Accepting his hand, she rose. Instantly, she found herself in his embrace. She hugged his waist and swayed to a music only they could hear. The pleasure of being held in his arms was almost overpowering. Breathing in his scent along with the crisp spring air, she tipped her head back, inviting a kiss. He didn't disappoint her.

"Matt?"

The sultry tone of her voice sent a shiver down his spine. "Yes, angel?"

"Are we going to sleep together tonight?"

Six

An indolent breeze rustled through the lacy canopy of trees sheltering the walkway to Matt's home. Moonlight filtered through the leaves. At the door Matt stopped and gently kissed Susan. Her mouth opened under his in an embrace as immediate and natural as the beginning of a brand-new day. "Are you real?" he asked, running his hands up and down her arms as though assuring himself she was truly there with him. "Or are you a dream?"

She feathered a kiss along his bottom lip. "If you're dreaming, so am I."

"Then let's be very quiet. I don't want to wake up and find myself alone." Placing a hand on each side of her face, he gazed into her eyes. "Are you sure, angel, this is what you want?"

She understood he was offering her the opportunity to change her mind. If she did, she knew he'd accept her decision with good grace. Another piece of the wall she'd built around her emotions crumbled.

"Very sure," she answered.

Matt could hear the certainty ringing true in her voice, could see it in her eyes. At last he'd won her consent to give their relationship a chance. Her trust touched him, and he vowed she'd have no cause for regrets.

"Come, angel," he said softly.

His smile stroked her as he captured her hand. Bone and muscle seemed to dissolve; she felt as if she were made solely of light and air.

They entered the house. Matt led her through the darkness to his bedroom. She stood on the threshold while he switched on a bedside lamp. As her eyes adjusted to the sudden illumination, she glanced around the room. It was spartan in appearance. The white walls were bare of decoration. A king-size four-poster took up most of the small room, an old-fashioned wardrobe swallowed up the rest. The only other furnishings were a table and lamp. Beyond an open doorway to her left, she spied an adjoining bath tiled in black and rose pink. The colors struck her as incongruent, considering the starkness of his bedroom. She wondered why nothing here conveyed Matt's personality.

"I want you," he whispered. "So much, I ache."

The desire in his voice rekindled her senses to life. She turned to the man standing beside the bed. The look in his eyes left her too emotion-filled to speak. Slowly, she went to him.

They stood close for a moment, not touching, simply content to feel the desire building between them. His breath wafted over her face. Her nails curled into her palms. With a fingertip he traced a pattern down her cheek to the pulse point below her jaw. Her heart rate increased. He smiled. She bit her bottom lip to keep it from trembling.

His eyes closed, he leaned his forehead on hers. "Susan, do you want to love me now? Say yes, my quicksilver angel."

"Yes." Unable to deny herself the pleasure of touching him any longer, she placed her hand over his heart. It beat wildly beneath her palm. "Quicksilver?"

she murmured, working his tie loose. She stripped it away and tossed it over her shoulder.

He caressed her shoulders, kissed her brow. "Because you're like quicksilver." He kicked off his shoes and she followed suit. "Totally unpredictable and impossible to hold."

Her soft laughter echoed in the quiet room. "Are you the same man who complained about my etched-in-stone schedule?" She eased the jacket from his shoulders and down his arms.

"You are unpredictable in other delightful ways." The coat fell to the floor. Threading his hands through her hair, he tilted her head back. "While I can still think like a responsible man, let me ask you a relative question."

Mischief sparkled in her eyes. "This isn't the time to talk about my relatives." His grin flashed briefly. She missed it when it was gone.

Laughter and delight fused inside him at the discovery of the playful side of her nature. "I love a woman who can keep her sense of humor in bed." He realized that falling in love with Susan was the best thing he had ever done. She made him happy. "What I'm trying to say is that I have protection if we need it."

Susan stopped unbuttoning his shirt. She'd been celibate for so long, the issue hadn't occurred to her. Her embarrassment passed quickly, though. "Thank you. You're a very nice man." Continuing with her task of removing his shirt, she smiled up at him. "Am I going to need my sense of humor in bed?"

"I certainly hope not." He bared one of her shoulders, then helped the gown slither to her hips. The sight of her breasts, covered only by an ivory chemise with a lace bodice, stole his breath. Swimming up through a lover's fog, he disciplined himself to go slowly, and stood still while she stripped away his shirt.

Sighing, Susan wrapped her arms around his waist, enjoying the warm, solid feel of him.

Matt closed his eyes as an explosion of sensations assailed him. For a moment he could only think of how wonderful it felt having her breasts pressed against his chest.

"Kiss me again, Matt," she ordered, an urgent need curling inside her as if it were a living thing.

"As you wish." He kissed her chin, then moved on to her mouth, provocatively stroking his tongue against hers. Pulling back, he wondered if he looked as dazed and flushed with longing as she did. The prelude to making love to a woman had never seemed so erotic. Gently tugging her dress past her slim hips, he watched in fascination as it fell in a glimmering pool around her feet.

"You still have on too many clothes," he said, touching his mouth to the hollow between her breasts.

His breath warmed her wherever it touched. Excitement quivered through her as he found the taut bud of her breast through the lace barrier. Susan felt a quickening response deep in the core of her body. Tilting her head, she explored the texture of his hair with her lips. "Matt," she entreated, "please hurry."

"There's no rush. We have all night."

"I know, but I can't wait to find out if I'll need my sense of humor."

"This," he murmured, returning to her lips, "is the beginning of a weird and wonderful relationship. I do believe *I* have on too many clothes. Why don't you help me?"

Her smile was at once sensual and artless. She almost rocked him off his feet as she trailed a string of kisses down his torso. His stomach muscles contracted with the touch of her tongue in his navel, and he felt himself going up in flames when she dropped to her knees. Her fingers performed magic with delicate caresses while she freed him of the remainder of his clothing. The need to touch her in kind overwhelmed him. In a skilled motion that elicited a soft gasp from her, he drew her leisurely up the length of his body. They added her chemise and stockings to the pile on the floor.

Matt swept the covers back, then slowly lowered her to his bed. Honey-blond hair fanned away from her pretty face and rested on his pillow like angel wings. His gaze traveled appreciatively over her slender, beautifully curved body. Carefully placing a hand on her gently rounded stomach, he felt it quiver beneath his palm. Her reaction, the satin-smooth skin, the look of his darker hand upon her creamy flesh, enchanted him. His hands grew bolder, gliding from hip to ankle, and he listened for her slight intakes of breath to reveal her most sensitive places. Looking into her eyes, he found total acceptance and the reflection of his own rising passion. She lifted her arms to him in a silent yet eloquent invitation. He allowed himself to be drawn down until his body completely covered hers. Heaven, he thought, burrowing his face in the curve of her neck. He was holding a little bit of heaven.

Susan closed her eyes as she absorbed his precious weight. They fit together so perfectly. Her senses tilted and spun. The world blurred. She gave herself up to the feeling of rightness.

They began a journey of total communication, learning to touch each other with tender sensuality, enjoying sight, feel, taste, and smell. She marveled that he accurately read her every response, seeming to know what pleased her as well as signaling his own needs. Drinking in the passion that flowed so freely between them, she felt her entire body throb under the gentle persuasion of his mouth on her breast. Instinctively, she held him closer, compelled by overwhelming need.

Matt ached from head to toe from wanting her. Her hands working magic on his sweat-dampened flesh was sweeter than a chorus of angels. Locking his hands at the base of her spine, he rolled over, taking her with him. She pulled back to look at him, and he wondered if she could see love shining in his eyes. If she did, would it frighten her away?

She stroked his face, then leaned down to kiss him, sending a shower of tresses onto his shoulder. He hugged her tight, as if he could pull her inside himself and hold her safe there.

Slowly she rose above him, and his name flowed from her kiss-swollen lips like a litany. Unable to bear not being a part of him any longer, she made them one, gasping as he filled her completely. Swirling colors formed behind her closed eyelids. He spoke to her in hushed lyrical words she didn't understand. As they moved together, their bodies perfectly attuned, their passions rising swiftly to a crescendo, she acknowledged deep inside herself that their bonding was one of soul, spirit, and heart.

"You'd look good in my shirt."

Sitting cross-legged on the bed, Susan started guiltily. Matt stood in the doorway watching her, wearing only a half smile. Feeling a bit awkward for getting caught hugging his castoff shirt, breathing in his lingering scent, she blushed, but smiled back.

Holding a tray loaded with a plastic bowl and two glasses of diet cola, he walked to the bed with easy grace. "Go ahead, put it on if you want. I rather like the idea of you wearing my shirt."

She pulled on the shirt, leaving it unbuttoned. Her color heightened further, for it seemed yet another act of intimacy.

"I love the way you blush at the least provocation." He settled the tray on the table, then crawled into bed beside her.

"I hate it," she said. "It makes me feel like a silly schoolgirl."

"I bet you were a sweet schoolgirl." His thumb

caressed her cheek. "I imagine you at Nikki's age, looking much like she does, only"—he grinned— "quieter."

Susan laughed. "I guess I was. I think I was much more naïve and innocent at her age, though. She amazes me sometimes. Nik's sensitive, but she's a tough little cookie, thank heaven."

Matt nodded, reaching for the bowl, piled high with fluffy popcorn. "That she is. Our Nikki knows her own mind."

His casual reference to her daughter as "our Nikki" took Susan aback momentarily, creating an odd feeling in her chest.

"She'll grow into a fine young woman," he continued, "who can tame life with one hand tied behind her back. Have some popcorn." He fed her a lightly popped kernel.

"I've never eaten popcorn in bed after making love." Or, she added silently, known the aftermath of making love could be almost as enjoyable.

"Neither have I," he said. "Isn't this fun?"

She dipped her hand into the bowl. "I thought you liked a ton of butter on your popcorn. So where's the butter?"

"That stuff's dangerous. Clogs up your arteries."

She raised an elegant eyebrow. "Don't tell me you're a health nut and your pantry's stocked with enough wheat germ and honey to survive a holocaust."

Laugh lines crinkled at the corners of his eyes. "Of course. I plan to serve you a double helping for breakfast." He laughed at the face she made. "I don't have a single grain of wheat germ in the house. I'm just fashionably health conscious." Slipping a hand inside the shirt, he placed it over her left breast, feeling the rhythmic beat of her heart come alive, loving her rapid intake of air. "Besides, your heartbeat is so beautiful, I wouldn't want to do anything to damage it."

Susan's gaze riveted to his deep-set eyes. Was this

his way of telling her he wasn't going to break her heart? Dear sweet man, she thought with an ever-quickening heartbeat throbbing in her ears. She leaned toward him, initiating a voluptuous, open-mouthed kiss. The bowl of popcorn lay between them, forgotten, as they savored the warmth and surging revival of desire.

Matt drew back, his muscles subtly tightening, reminding him it didn't take much to rekindle the passion that seemed to come so quickly and easily to them. A touch, a glance, and he wanted her all over again. So very tempting. For now, he just wanted to be with her, talk with her, perhaps hold her. "Tell me your secrets," he said, smoothing her brow with a finger.

She cocked her head to one side, looking at him uncertainly. "What do you mean? I don't have any secrets."

"Sure you do." He poked through the popcorn, searching out the few that were slightly burnt. "Everybody has secrets. Not great big secrets, just little ones. Things you do, or like, or think about, but won't tell anybody else because you think they'll laugh."

"For instance," she demanded.

He showed her the burnt popcorn in his hand. "I always eat the singed ones first. For some reason I like them best. Sometimes I leave the bag in the microwave a bit longer than necessary just to burn it a little."

"That isn't weird. I like the burnt ones too."

"So tell me your secrets, angel mine."

She released an exaggerated sigh. "All right, but you go first."

"Okay." He reached back to the table for the glasses, handing her one. "I love this set of glasses. Know why?"

As far as she could see, the tumbler was nothing

special. Just ordinary glass in an octagonal shape. She shook her head. "Why?"

"Because there's a word written on the bottom. The word is *turkey*. Actually, it says 'Made in Turkey', but the 'Made In' is very small and *Turkey* is printed in great big letters. So when you finish your drink, the word *Turkey* kind of jumps out at you. I'll never have to orally insult another person as long as I live. All I have to do is invite them home for a drink and let the bottom of the glass speak for me."

She held her tumbler up to peer at the bottom, and saw it was true. Squinting, she could see "Made In" hovering in tiny letters above the larger word.

"At the moment," he said, "it's my favorite private joke."

Susan glanced up. Her shoulders began to shake, and she laughed, more over the impish delight sparkling in his eyes than the punch line on the bottom of the glass. "You're right. Can I borrow them? I want to invite Rachel Henderson over for a glass of iced tea."

"Did she pinch your cheeks, too, when you were a kid?"

"Lord, yes."

He kissed the tip of her nose. "Borrow them anytime. Okay, that's two. I'll confess a couple more, then it's your turn. I gave my sister away at her wedding and embarrassed her all the way down the aisle by sniffling back tears. Cara said I sounded like I had a head cold and walked as if I had ants in my pants. I can outcurse a sailor in six different languages, but speak only one fluently."

"I wouldn't laugh at any of those things. Except maybe at the ants in the pants."

For a moment, she studied him carefully, the thick black hair flowing smoothly to his nape, the chiseled, well-lived face, the lean, harmonious quality of bone structure, the soulful eyes, and that incredible smile. He was intelligent as well as handsome in his diamond-in-the-rough kind of way. His innate kindness appealed to her. Yet she had a feeling he would make a formidable enemy if he chose. She turned her head to look at the wall. No man had ever taken her to the heights of her own sensuality the way he had, or fed her popcorn in bed, or cared enough to pry into her whimsical secrets. A smile, lit from within, curved her mouth. She glanced back and found him munching popcorn, his expression solemn and intent, as though he were waiting for her to impart the secrets of the universe.

Delving into the recesses of her mind, she pulled out a bit of whimsy she knew he would appreciate—and tease her unmercifully with for the rest of her life. "I read romantic suspense novels in the bathtub with the door locked," she admitted, flushing a rosy pink.

"No!" He pretended to be overcome with shock. "Really, Susan, a pragmatist like you reads romance novels on the sly?"

"I like the suspense part," she claimed loftily, as some men might allege they only read the articles in sexy magazines.

"Sure you do," he teased. "Maybe we can read one together sometime." He lowered his voice. "In the bathtub. With the door locked."

"If you ever repeat that, I'll drown you in the bathtub. With the door locked." She drank some of the cola, then handed it to him to put back on the table.

"I'll take your torrid secret to my grave," he vowed. "Tell me more."

"I'm a secret chocoholic and I keep a bag of M & M's stashed in an old shoebox on the top shelf of my closet. I love the sound of rain hitting my bedroom window late at night. Greeting-card commercials make me tearfully sentimental, but I pretend I've got something in my eyes and rub them before anyone notices. Did your parents teach you to speak Italian?"

"No. I picked up a few words and phrases at

home . . . and a lot of curses." Seeing a flash of sympathy in her eyes, Matt swallowed irritation at himself and her. He wanted a lot of things from Susan Wright, but sympathy wasn't one of them. Never that.

"It's difficult for you to talk about yourself and your family, isn't it?" she said.

He blinked, and in that rapid eye movement Susan thought she detected strong emotion.

"I'm just not very good at it." He tossed off the rest of his drink and deposited the empty glass on the beside table. "Haven't had much practice," he added with a shrug.

"You can practice on me." Her hand crept up to his cheek, and he turned his head to kiss her palm.

His gaze roamed her face. "What do you want to know, the nice stuff or the garbage?"

"Anything." She shifted, leaning back against the headboard. "Everything."

"My parents were second-generation Italian-Americans. I was born in the same part of Chicago where they grew up. It was a classic melting pot, predominantly Italian, Polish, and Irish with a smattering of other nationalities tossed in for good measure. When she was a child, according to Mama, it was a community of hardworking people in search of the American dream. By the time I came along, it was well on its way to becoming a slum." Matt's bland tone of voice changed with the onset of half-forgotten memories. "In our six-floor apartment building, I could identify the nationality of the occupants of each flat from the cooking smells seeping through their door."

His eyes clouded. "I didn't know my father very well, nor did I want to. He was an alcoholic. Couldn't keep a job. He would disappear for months at a time. All of sudden, he'd show up at home, stinkin' drunk, mean, and looking for a fight." Matt smiled ruefully. "That's how I learned to curse fluently in Italian and sidestep a punch in the face. He disappeared for good when I was about nine. We were relieved, to say the least. Cara was only four. She has little memory of him, thank God."

"Is he still alive?"

"I have no idea, but given his life-style, I rather doubt it."

"Tell me about your mother and Cara," she urged softly.

He smiled. "Paolina, my mother, and Cara were the nice part. Mama was beautiful, the most gentle woman I've ever known. She was barely five feet tall, weighed maybe ninety pounds soaked to the skin, hair black as coal until the day she died. She was always singing and laughing at home, unless my father was there. Then she was quiet, as if afraid anything she said or did might put him in a rage. I hated him for that. I asked her once why she didn't kick the s.o.b. out on his tail. She said because he was her husband and she remembered too well the boy he used to be. Didn't make any sense to me. It still doesn't."

By his pensive frown, Susan could see it bothered him greatly. She slipped her hand into his. "Perhaps your mother saw something very good in him and refused to give up."

"Maybe," he said in a flat voice. "Want to hear something weird? Although I was relieved when he left, I was also angry at him for abandoning us."

"I can understand your feelings. It's only natural for a child to have conflicting emotions in such a situation. Tell me more about you mother."

A fond smile again lightened his expression. "She worked days in a bakery and nights for a cleaning service. Education was important to her. She left school after the eighth grade. Her greatest ambition was for her children to attend college and have a better life. Money was always tight, but every payday she'd take us to the bank and deposit whatever she could into a savings account. I started picking up odd jobs to help her as soon as I was old enough."

He paused and glanced at Susan, grinning. "The best-paying job I ever had as a kid was illegal as hell. When I was seven, I worked for a bookmaker who ran numbers out of the pool hall around the corner from our apartment. Only had the job for a week before Mama found out and went through the roof. I'll never forget her grabbing me by the arm and dragging me down there to confront the guy. She blistered his hide, telling him what she thought of hooligans who corrupt innocent children." He laughed. "I can still see his meaty face sweating. She made me give the money back too."

Susan smiled, but her heart bled for him. It was difficult for her to imagine that he'd come from a background so fraught with violence and abuse. Her childhood was the antithesis of his. "Your mother sounds like she was a woman of quiet dignity and courage." From the warmth in his eyes, she knew she'd said the right thing.

"Thank you. Cara inherited all of Mama's best qualities. I look at her and I believe she's what Mama would have been if given the opportunity. Do you want some more popcorn?"

Susan shook her head. Thinking about the things he'd told her, he rose in her esteem. She remembered him saying his sister was a graphic artist, and she didn't need to be told that he was the one who'd made his mother's dream of educating her children come true.

He returned the half-empty bowl to the tray. "I really don't want to talk about it anymore tonight." His voice faded to a hushed stillness. He lay down and gathered her in his embrace.

"What were the words you said to me when we were making love?" she asked. "Were they Italian?" She wedged a hand between their bodies. Her heart started to beat in sync with his.

He stroked her hair, whispering against her ear in Italian and English. "*Tu sei bellissima.* You are very beautiful. *Sono in balian te.* I am at your mercy."

She quickened to his touch.

"*Mia bell' angela.* My lovely angel."

A floating blend of excitement and tenderness carried her to an emotional peak.

"*Fare l'amore,* making love with you is, *beatitudine,* bliss." Silently, he added the one phrase he would not translate for her, not yet. *Ti amo molto.* I love you very much.

Seven

"Matt, we can't do that in the shower."

"Sure we can. Just takes a little imagination and . . . uh, creativity. My, but you're slippery."

Susan wrapped herself around him. Steam rose from the cascading hot water, yet the black tile against her back felt cool. "You're going to drop me. I just know it. I'll break a leg and—"

He covered her mouth with his.

Flames licked through her veins. She felt as if she were drowning in a sea of passion. The thought struck her as hilarious. Jerking her head away, she began to laugh.

"What's so funny?"

"Drowning," she gasped. "In a sea of passion."

"Huh?"

"Never mind. I'd better go home before I wind up in the emergency room." Her body was screaming for more, but her brain was turning to mush.

"You can't leave now," he said. "Life's just getting interesting. Besides, Dellie as good as told us to dance until dawn."

"It's almost dawn," she told him, kissing his wet shoulder.

"That's true. But I'm not through dancing. Hold still, angel mine. I think . . . I think . . . Oh, yes."

Feeling as if a goofy smile were permanently fixed upon his face, Matt attended church with Susan and her family on Sunday. Afterwards, he eagerly accepted an invitation to spend the rest of the day at the Simpson house. He knew, with Dellie and Nikki there, he and Susan wouldn't have the opportunity to repeat the previous night's ecstasy. Any time he spent with her was fine with him, though. So he was disappointed when, after lunch and without looking at him, Susan apologetically excused herself to work in her office.

Slipping her small hand into his, Nikki took him up to the attic. They cranked up the Victrola and listened to the tinny sound of a waltz as she introduced him to the treasures haphazardly stored there.

"My birthday is the first week of May," she said as she placed a silk top hat on his head.

"Great! How old are you going to be? Sixteen?"

She looked up from the trunk she was pawing through and giggled. "Noooo, silly. Eleven."

Matt noticed for the first time how much bluer her eyes were than her mother's.

"Mom's letting me have a birthday slumber party."

"You're going to sleep on your birthday?" he asked seriously.

"Nooo! We're going to dress up and dance and talk all night. Isn't that simply fabulous?" She barely gave him time to nod before rushing on. "Billie Jo will be here for the party. Mom won't let her bring her dog, though. She's my best friend in the whole world. Billie Jo, not her dog," she clarified. "We're totally different, but we like the same things. She's the tiniest little girl in my class. She's sort of quiet and lets me decide what kind of games we'll play. I can't keep my mouth shut for more than five minutes.

Silence drives me crazy. It's always silent in our house. I love being at Billie Jo's house. It's filled with people and pets. It's never quiet there." She paused as though she'd just made a connection she'd never thought of before. "Maybe that's why she likes silence so much."

Nikki's sweet and confiding manner gripped Matt's heart, and her rapid-fire speech and innocent-wise view of the world kept him on the verge of laughter. He reached in the trunk and pulled out a red feather boa. "I guess we always want something we don't have," he said solemnly, looping the boa around the child's shoulders.

She peered up at him intently. "Have you ever desperately wanted something you couldn't have?"

"Yes."

"So have I. What did you wish for when you were my age?"

Matt considered the question carefully. There was only one thing he could remember wishing for at ten. The wish had eventually come true, but it had arrived years too late. "I wanted to be rich," he said, "so my mother wouldn't have to work so hard."

Nikki sighed. "I know what you mean. My mom works a lot. But she's always around for the important things, so I guess that's okay. It's just that sometimes . . ." For once, she didn't finish a sentence, but simply sat back and subjected him to a thoughtful stare. "Will you come to my birthday slumber party?"

"Do I have to wear pajamas?"

She erupted into giggles. "Nooo! Be here for pizza and cake. And wear that T-shirt that says 'I refuse to have a battle of wits with an unarmed person.' It's my favorite. Do you play poker?"

He grinned. "I played a hand or two in my misspent youth."

For the next two hours he sat at the kitchen table being tortured by the delicious smell of a slowly

cooking rib roast, and engaging in a fiercely compet-
itive poker game with a seventy-two-year-old woman
and a soon-to-be-eleven-year-old girl. He left the table
in debt to the tune of a million imaginary dollars and
the promise of his firstborn child.

Later, Matt sat with Susan on the Simpsons' porch
swing, content with the slow, drifting pace and the
sunset. The sky blazed with color like a laser light
show, molten gold streaking and swirling with a haze
of pink, orange, and purple-blue.

Sighing happily, Susan rested her head on his
shoulder.

He wrapped his arms more securely around her,
loving the way her silky hair felt against his cheek.
He found her more fascinating and alluring by the
minute. She was intelligent and humorous, confident one minute, shy the next. She was the center of
her family's gravity. He admired the way she viewed
their idiosyncrasies with tolerance and patience,
loving and respecting them unconditionally.

"Why are you here?" she asked.

The question caught him off guard. "Why am I
here? Because I want to be with you. I could get used
to cuddling with you every night on this swing."

"Me too," she said with a smile. "But I meant, why
are you in Millers Creek? What can a small town like
this offer a city-bred man like you?"

"It's a good place for a video store?"

"I'm serious. We roll up the sidewalks at ten o'clock.
The brightest light in town comes from the movie
theater marquee, and it's turned off at eleven. Not
exactly what you're used to. What's the attraction?"

"Peace," he answered, unable to keep his voice as
casual as he intended. "A new life. No traffic jams. No
hassles."

"What about your friends? Don't you miss them?"

"I don't have any close friends. Good acquaintances,

yes. But no one I miss, or who misses me. Never had time for that sort of thing before." He glanced at her. "You're looking at me as if you're not sure you believe me."

"I believe you. I'm surprised, that's all. You seem to have a knack for making people like you. You already have friends here."

Amazement then pleasure swept across his face. "I do?"

She nodded. "That's why I assumed you left a lot behind in Chicago."

"It's easy to get to know people in this town," he said slowly. "Everybody speaks or smiles at one another on the street. The first time I visited here to check the location, I was taken aback by the number of strangers who said hello to me. In the city, we barely look at anyone in passing. It's a great feeling to know I can walk down Main Street and meet at least one person who'll wish me a good morning."

Susan laughed. "We have to be friendly. This town's so small, we live in one another's pockets."

"You love it here. Why shouldn't I?"

"Yes, I do now. But there was a time when I couldn't wait to get away."

"So you went to college. Did you always want to be an accountant?"

She looked up at him, amusement glittering in her eyes. "Matt, have you ever heard any kid express a desire to be an accountant?"

He grinned. "Can't say I have. What did you want to be?"

"I," she said grandly, "was going to be the next Picasso."

His eyebrows shot up in surprise. "An artist? You're kidding." Never in a million years would he have guessed that one.

She chuckled. "That's exactly what my art professor said."

"How'd you get from art to accounting?"

"Pure luck, I guess."

"Why did you give up your art?"

She sighed. "All my life I was sheltered and loved, and I grew up thinking I was smart and talented. Someone pretty special." A self-deprecating smile flitted over her features. "I wanted to be an artist from the first box of watercolors Dellie gave me for Christmas when I was four. I went off to college believing I was destined to be a great painter, and was one step away from flying off to Paris, where I'd live in a garret and starve for my art like all the great ones. One day I wandered around my painting class comparing my work with the others. All of sudden I was struck by the sheer genius radiating from some of the canvases. They were alive. These artists had looked at the same thing I had, but they'd filtered it through their emotions, internalized it. They'd interpreted that vision with paint. I went back to my painting and honestly evaluated it. I didn't have that kind of inner vision. Technically, my painting was good, but it lacked that inner spark that makes a painting a true work of art. I realized I was a mediocre artist. And mediocrity was simply unacceptable."

He stroked her shoulder sympathetically. "I can imagine how that must have hurt."

She shrugged. "I rarely think about it anymore. Math was my second love, so the switch seemed natural. I'm not pining away for youthful dreams. My job is very satisfying. I'm good at it. My only regret is that I didn't have the maturity to accept my limitations as an artist. Instead, I rejected it completely. And that's too bad. Painting would have been an enjoyable hobby. Then again, I don't have time for hobbies these days."

Matt's thoughts kept him busy for a moment. Was that her streak of practicality speaking? Had it been so easy for her to dismiss a lifetime dream? Or had she merely convinced herself it was no big deal? Intuition, and a basic knowledge of how Susan

Wright's mind worked, told him she was simply good at denying her own feelings. He decided to dig a little deeper. "Why did a nice pragmatist like you marry a music man?"

Susan's mouth went dry. Her stomach knotted. "That's a good question. I've often asked myself the same thing." Her laughter rang hollow. "Just young and stupid, I suppose. In love with love. Brian was handsome, exciting, never serious about anything. He was different from anyone I'd ever known. And . . ." She lapsed into a reflective silence, then haltingly expressed feelings she'd never put into words before. "I think I was impressed with his gift for music. Somehow, his talent made up for the lack of mine. The problem was I had drive and ambition, but no talent. Brian had talent, but no motivation. He believed he'd just wake up someday and be a superstar."

Matt didn't want to ask, but he needed to know about her past. It was important to get the past out of the way so they could get on with their future. "Is that what went wrong with your marriage?"

"Partly." Susan peered beyond the veranda. Darkness was beginning to shadow the trees. Only faint colors were left on the horizon. "When we were first married, I thought traveling would be thrilling. It didn't take long for it to wear thin. I hated living in cheap hotels, sitting night after night in beer joints and teen bars, listening to the band, waiting for my husband to shoo away the groupie types that inhabit such places. Once Nikki was on the way, I stationed myself in Atlanta. I went to school during the day and waited on tables at night. Brian sent postcards from Miami, New Orleans, Dallas, and a dozen other cities. He was in San Francisco when Nikki was born. She was eight months old before he saw her." Susan's lips thinned with anger. "He treated her like a neat new toy. Fun to play with until the novelty wears off. That was the beginning of the end for me. It was truly over when I found him in bed with his new lead singer."

Matt's arm tightened around her shoulders. His heart went out to the young woman who'd discovered how fragile the bonds of love could be. Understanding how her trust had been betrayed and how disillusioned she must have felt, he valued her trust in him all the more. "What a bum," he said, angry on her behalf. "If he were here, I'd kick his tail all the way to China."

Her sentiments exactly. She turned to kiss Matt's chin.

Cupping her face in his hands, he murmured against her lips, "The poor slob didn't know what he was throwing away. You deserve to be loved and cherished."

Lost in the intimate duel of the kiss, they didn't see the two grinning faces pressed against the parlor window.

Over the next two weeks, Matt and Susan's relationship developed into a daily routine. Every morning Matt jogged by the Simpson house and stopped to breakfast with the family. He and Susan often met for lunch at Walker's. He dined with the family at the Red Dragon on Fridays, attended church with them on Sundays. They went to aerobics together. Three nights a week he taught Dellie the art of Italian cuisine.

The two of them spent Saturdays alone together. They toured the Moravian village in Old Salem. She taught him to roller-skate. He gave her the grand tour of his video store and proudly demonstrated his state-of-the art computer equipment.

One evening Susan was in her office, trying to keep her mind on an article about tax-exempt bonds. After reading the same paragraph four times, she quit and listened to the sound of Matt's voice and Nikki's giggles coming from the family room. Although Matt had been wonderful about respecting her work habits, he was constantly in her thoughts and in her house.

Sighing, she picked up a pencil and poked it into the electric sharpener. So far, she hadn't allowed herself to think beyond the moment. Matt filled an empty slot in her life—for now.

One of the things she enjoyed most was relaxing with him on the porch swing after dinner and talking over the day's events. Sometimes they shared memories about growing up, painful ones as well as silly incidents that stuck in their minds. His stories about his mother, and how he'd often felt lost and inadequate when raising his teenage sister alone, brought tears to her eyes. She admired his inner strength to survive. And she told him things about her marriage that she'd never spoken aloud to anyone. She loved the way he discussed his plans for the promotional video for Millers Creek with her and took her suggestions seriously.

Everything was going great, so why was she sitting there, nerves jangled and feeling confused? Susan absently lifted the pencil and used the eraser to scratch the hive on the underside of her jaw. Frowning, she looked at the pencil. She'd sharpened it to a stub. "Oh, good grief." She tossed it away.

She was being drawn into Matt's life every bit as much as he was infiltrating hers. He was changing her in little ways, and she had no control over the way he touched her emotions. She realized they were both slowly peeling away their outer layers, opening themselves up, becoming vulnerable. She wasn't sure she liked the feeling. Vulnerable was scary. The possibilities for being hurt were all too great.

Susan got up and headed for the family room. Maybe she needed to rein herself in a bit. After all, the idea was to let him in her life just a little, not invite him to take over. She heard his laughter float out into the hall. Exercising caution wasn't going to be easy, she thought wryly, when the man was practically living in her house.

She stopped at the threshold of the family room. Matt and Nikki were sitting on the floor in front of the coffee table, which was littered with textbooks and papers. They were working on math word problems. He appeared to be as thrilled as the child over the solution to a particularly tricky question. Her daughter's face glowed from his praise.

Susan couldn't help feeling envious. Nikki didn't respond to her tutoring attempts half as well. Their sessions always ended in frustration. On occasion, she'd snapped impatiently at the child, making Nikki cry. In all honesty, she was glad Matt succeeded where she failed. But it would be nice if she were the one to spark such enthusiasm in her own daughter.

She could see that Nikki was becoming more attached to Matt every day. She stuck to him like a leech, following him around the house, talking nonstop. It hadn't escaped Susan's notice that Nikki was telling him things about her friends and about events at school that she usually reserved for bedtime chats with her mother. She ran that observation through her emotional maze and found it hurt her feelings . . . a little.

Fixing a smile on her face, she went to join them.

The night of Nikki's birthday party arrived. Matt stood on the front porch, wearing a lopsided grin, and balancing a wiggly puppy and a shopping bag. He heard high-pitched squeals and giggles coming from inside the house.

For a moment he savored his own happiness. Happiness, he mused, wasn't something that came in a great big lump. In his book, it was made up of lots of little events that happened to fall into place when least expected. The last few weeks had been like that, with many small and insignificant events falling perfectly into place. The feeling of belonging, of finally coming home, awed him.

Thank heaven he'd had the good sense to leave Chicago and move there to meet Susan Wright in an elementary school parking lot. Every day he fell deeper in love with her. He wanted to be a part of her hopes and dreams and future. He smiled, thinking it was only a matter of time before they naturally progressed to a serious commitment.

The puppy whimpered.

"It's okay, pal," he said soothingly. "This is your new home. It isn't always this noisy around here, I promise. There's a little girl inside who needs you as much as you need her. Her name is Nikki and she'll give you lots of love and affection. You may not realize it yet, but you are one lucky dog."

The puppy looked up at him. Flicking out a wet tongue, he licked Matt's wrist.

"Save the soulful eyes and cute puppy charm for Susan, pal. It's her you'll have to win over."

Whimpering again, the puppy burrowed his head in the crook of Matt's arm, until he appeared to be a furry white muff with legs and a big red bow.

"Don't worry, little guy. She has a generous spirit. Once she gets used to you, she'll love you. It took her a while to get used to me, but she did. And I'm not half as cute and cuddly as you." Matt pressed a thumb to the doorbell. He couldn't wait for Nikki to meet her present.

He heard a shout. Feet—lots of feet—thundered through the foyer.

Nikki flung the door open. She was backed by a dozen or so girls. "Matt!" she screeched, then giggled. "I thought you'd never get—" Her mouth dropped open as she caught sight of the puppy.

Matt watched an expression of wonder glaze the child's eyes. Her reaction went straight to his heart.

He set the bag down, then placed the puppy in her arms. "Happy birthday, *carissima*."

Nikki reverently held the puppy. Black button eyes stared solemnly at her. A smile of pure joy parted her lips. "Mine?" she finally breathed. "Really mine? To keep forever and ever?"

Matt nodded.

"Thank you!" She threw herself, puppy and all, at him, capturing him for a hug. "I'll take care of him. I promise. Look," she shouted, turning to her friends. "Doesn't he have the sweetest face?"

Pandemonium broke out among the horde of girls. They moved in, trying to pat the little dog and cooing: "He looks just like a teddy bear." "He needs a name." "Can I hold him?" "Ew ew ew! He licked my face!" "Shut up, it's just puppy kisses!"

Drawn by the noise, Susan came out of the kitchen and into the foyer. She saw Matt sitting cross-legged on the floor, looking happy and right at home surrounded by the children. He glanced up and gave her one of his million-dollar grins that always took her breath away. Her responding smile froze.

Her daughter was cradling a fuzzy creature in her arms. Susan's eyes widened, then narrowed in dismay.

It couldn't be. *Oh, please, let it be a stuffed toy.*

The thing moved. Its mouth gaped open in a sleepy yawn, displaying a pink tongue and rows of tiny baby teeth. Teeth that would be replaced by bigger teeth. Strong, healthy teeth capable of eating her best shoes. Teeth that could bite.

No, it wasn't a toy. It was a . . . *dog.*

She flashed Matt an accusing glare that said "this is all your fault, you rat." He returned it with one that said "oops."

"Mom!" Nikki exclaimed. "Look what Matt gave me. It's a puppy! Matt says it's a Lhasa apso. I'm going to name him Teddy Bear. Isn't he simply fabulous?"

"Divine," she answered in a dry tone. "Go show it to

Dellie. No doubt she'll be thrilled." Susan had a feeling her life from now on was going to be pure hell.

Nikki sprang to her feet and rushed toward the kitchen with her new treasure. The other children ran after her.

Matt quickly grabbed the shopping bag he'd left by the door and tried to slink past Susan. She looked like she wanted to chew him up and spit him out.

She grabbed a fistful of his shirt. "May I speak to you, Mr. Martinelli? In private." Not giving him a choice, she dragged him down the hall.

"I'm in trouble, huh?" he said as she pushed him into her office and slammed the door.

"You don't know how much. Sit down. And don't you dare look at me that way."

"What way?"

"Like . . . you know. Like you want to kiss me. I'm angry and I don't want to lose it. So cut it out, Romeo."

"I do want to kiss you, angel." With effort, he held his laughter at bay. "But I won't. You're mad and you don't want to lose it." He headed for the leather chair by the fireplace and made himself at home. "Okay. Go for the kill."

"Don't be amused at me, Mr. Martinelli. You know I don't want a dog in this house, and yet you waltz in here and give my child one. Why did you do that?"

"Why don't you like dogs, angel?"

"They shed. They chew up the furniture and anything else they can sink their teeth into." Warming to the subject, Susan paced in front of her desk. "They're expensive. Did you know it costs more to take a dog to the vet than your child to a pediatrician? And they eat tons. The thrill of taking care of it will wear off in a week for Nikki. Then Dellie and I will be stuck taking care of that—that thing. My aunt is seventy-two years old. What if she falls over it and breaks a hip?" She flopped down on the edge of the desk. Arms crossed over her chest, she glared at him.

A light of understanding flicked on in Matt's mind. "You're afraid of dogs."

"Oh, please," she snorted. "Me, afraid of a little puppy?"

The look in her eyes told him all he needed to know. He stood up and slowly walked toward her. "You are scared of dogs. That's why you don't want Nikki to have one."

Susan's gaze dropped to the floor. "I'm not scared of them. I just don't like them."

Capturing her chin in his hand, he gently raised her face. "Look at me and tell me that."

"All right. I'm afraid of dogs. It's no big deal. Lots of people are afraid of dogs. They bite, you know."

With her lower lip jutting forward in a pout, she looked just like her daughter in one of her rare snits. He couldn't laugh. Her fear was real. He kissed her as tenderly as a mother might kiss a newborn infant. "I'm sorry, angel. I didn't realize you felt that way. Forgive me. I only knew Nikki wanted a pet very badly. I passed by the pet shop today, saw the puppy, and couldn't resist buying him for her. I wanted to make her happy. I didn't mean to make you unhappy in the process."

"It isn't your job to make my child happy."

"I know it isn't," he said, wishing otherwise. "Do you want me to return the puppy?"

Susan closed her eyes. The image of her daughter lovingly cradling the dog flashed behind her eyelids. "No. It would break her heart. We'll keep it." She glanced up at him. "But don't ever do anything like that again without talking to me first."

Framing her face in his hands, he kissed her again, deeply, enjoying the texture and taste of her mouth. Her instant response warmed him. She gave without reservation, wrapping her arms around his waist. Raining kisses over her face, he made a sound that was half laugh, half groan. "There's a birthday party going on out there. I don't suppose this is the time or place to get too involved, huh?"

She stroked back the hair that covered his ear and kissed his cheek. "No, it isn't."

"Do girls actually sleep at slumber parties?"

Her soft laugh feathered against his face. "Never. The purpose of a slumber party is to stay up all night."

"I was afraid you were going to say that. I think I'd better let you go before I no longer care if we get caught in a very compromising position. Besides, I have a present for you too."

"A ton of puppy food?" she asked, releasing him.

"That's still in the Jag." He took her hand and led her over to the leather chair, then picked up the shopping bag. "This is something just for you." He lowered her into the chair and set the bag on her lap.

Susan peered inside it. There were several wrapped packages, two flat ones and one big square box. She glanced curiously at him.

He lifted them out and handed her one. "Open it."

Carefully removing the paper and ribbon, she lifted the lid. A slow smile crept over her lips as she viewed the contents. Paints. Dozens of tubes of paints. Acrylics. Oils. Watercolors. Brushes. With trembling fingers, she reverently picked up a tube of cadmium red. The passion she'd once known echoed through her. It began singing in her veins. The feel of a brush in her hand. The rich smell of paint. An unblemished canvas waiting to be filled with form and color. It all came back to her in a dizzy rush.

She looked up at him. He was perched on the chair arm, waiting so still and silent for her reaction. A tear sparkled on her eyelashes. "I don't know what to say. Except thank you."

"Say you'll paint something for me."

At four A.M. Susan tiptoed into the family room, where Nikki and her guests were camped out in sleeping bags. Not a soul stirred. She wished Matt could see the transformation from wired-for-sound hellions to sleeping cherubs. She grinned, remembering his observation that Nikki was entering the "yo-yo" stage of having one foot in Pee-Wee's playhouse and the other in melodramatic adolescence. "Face it, Susan," he'd teased, "the teenage years are coming. From now on neither your life nor Nikki's will ever be the same."

A bittersweet wistfulness crept over her. She couldn't keep Nikki from growing up and changing. Nor did she want to. It gave her an incredible feeling of satisfaction to know her child was forming her own identity and developing into a strong, capable individual. Her goal was to raise her daughter to be the kind of woman who could go out into the world and meet it on her own terms. So far, Susan thought she'd done a good job. She'd be able to let go when the time came. But, she acknowledged, a part of her did want to hold on to her baby.

Gingerly stepping over sleeping children, she tucked each child in. She removed headphones from a curly-haired imp, an empty potato chip bag from the slack fist of one, a teen magazine from another.

She saved Nikki for last. Kneeling down, she brushed back the lustrous curtain of hair covering her child's face. Nikki sighed and smiled happily in her sleep. Susan kissed her forehead.

Something cold and wet touched her cheek. She shot upward, biting back a startled cry. It was that *thing*. Round liquid eyes stared into hers. It wiggled out of the sleeping bag and nudged her with its nose. She shivered involuntarily. "You're supposed to be locked in the bathroom, you mangy mutt," she whispered. Her stomach lurched at the thought of picking it up to put it back where it belonged.

It made a whimpering baby sound, and propped two white paws on her knee. Its eyes seemed to plead for affection.

Sitting on her heels, Susan dispassionately studied the puppy. It wasn't completely white. Its ears were tipped with black and tan. So was the curling tail that flipped back and forth. The animal's coat appeared soft and silky. And it did sort of look like a teddy bear with a goatee.

"It's just a puppy. A harmless puppy," she murmured. Nothing like the big German shepherd that had knocked her down and sat on her chest, baring its teeth and growling in her terrified six-year-old face. She still bore the scar on her forearm where the dog had ripped her flesh before its owner had dragged it away.

Just a puppy. She lifted a tentative hand. Gulping in a ragged breath, she patted the shaggy head. Its coat felt as sleek and luxurious as it looked. Going a step further, she stroked its back. The dog sighed contentedly as it gazed up at her with adoring eyes. It wiggled its warm little body up her leg.

Just a small and helpless puppy. Instinctively, Susan drew him into her arms. "You're only a baby, aren't you?" she said as the dog snuggled into her embrace. There was no way this sweet little scrap of fur was going to grow up to be a killer hound.

She smiled and rubbed her cheek against Teddy Bear's silky head.

By midmorning on Saturday, all the children had departed to their respective homes with the exception of Billie Jo Brown. Susan was in her office catching up on paperwork she'd neglected the day before in order to help Dellie prepare for the birthday party.

Satisfied she'd accomplished enough for the time being, she closed the ledger she was working on, then stood up and stretched. She wandered over to the window and leaned against the wall to look out.

Beyond the veranda, wrapping around the three-story Victorian house, was Dellie's garden. Mountain laurel, azaleas, forsythias, scarlet firethorn pyracantha, climbing roses, dogwood trees, and evergreen shrubs lent privacy and an intimate charm to the area. In the center, Matt sat with Dellie on a stone bench. They were contentedly surveying her great-aunt's colorful fairylike kingdom.

Susan smiled affectionately as she noted her aunt's face held its usual expression, a serenity as peaceful as the garden itself. Dellie's posture-perfect figure seemed as delicate as the peonies she grew.

Her gaze swung lazily to Matt. He'd arrived in time for breakfast with the kids, and had been gardening with Dellie since nine. She shook her head, grinning. He looked like a field hand come to do the bidding of the lady of the manor.

Worn jeans with the suggestion of threadbare knees hung low on his hips. He was bare-chested, having stripped off the red T-shirt and tossed it down carelessly beside the bench. Corded muscles and a fine sprinkling of dark, curling hair glistened with sweat in the warm sunlight. He appeared to be listening intently to Dellie, who was no doubt lecturing on the rhyme, reason, and careful preparation involved in planning a garden.

Just then Nikki ran past the window, blond plaits flying behind her. Legs and arms, already showing a healthy golden glow, churned like windmills. Teddy Bear loped along beside her. A tiny red-haired sprite, Billie Jo Brown, brought up the rear of the trio. All three swarmed on Matt.

He stood and caught Nikki around the waist as she made a dive for him. Susan heard her daughter's high-pitched squeals of delight as she was tossed up in the air and held suspended. The puppy yelped and hopped in circles around Matt's ankles. Billie Jo, shy and quiet as a mouse in church, gazed up at the pair with big eyes and a sweet smile.

What's wrong with this picture?

The thought came from nowhere, blind-siding the smile off Susan's face. Her eyes shut pensively. Patiently, analytically, she picked threads from the tangled skein in her mind.

The children. The dog. The grandmother type. The *daddy*. All frolicking harmoniously in the garden. Mommy looking on fondly from the window.

It was an illusion.

She shook her head sadly. An illusion like happily-ever-after endings, yet one she wanted to hang on to for however long it lasted. But it would end eventually. It was only a matter of time.

As wonderful as he was, she couldn't let herself forget that Matt wasn't the right man for her. He was a man who lived by his own rules, marched to different music. He wore his hair a little too long, preferred well-worn jeans and crazy tennis shoes, favored T-shirts with slogans over button-down oxfords, and ignored his business to romance her.

"Don't try to make me over in your own image," he'd said to her the week before when she'd tried to encourage him to show more interest in his video store. He'd laughingly dismissed the the suggestion of opening a second store in the next town, saying, "I'm happy with the one I've got, angel. It's comfortable, controllable. I want to enjoy life, not constantly worry over profit margins." That was Matt, all right. Happy with the status quo.

No, their fascination for each other couldn't last. She really didn't expect it to, no matter how much she wished to the contrary.

She opened her eyes and focused on the note taped to the closed office door. *Porta*. Dellie had declared that they would all learn to speak Italian, and had spent hours attaching labels written in her neat-flowing hand to furniture, appliances, or whatever. Both Dellie and Nikki had embraced Matt like a long-lost member of the family.

Would he leave not one but three broken hearts, she wondered, and a houseful of labels when he became bored with it all? She knew an idyllic scene of country life was painted inside his head. It would never stand the test of time. His Norman Rockwell view of Millers Creek would eventually pale.

Knuckles rapped on the window. She turned. Matt's face was pressed against the glass, his once-broken nose flat. His eyes bulged like a startled carp's and he made wide-lipped fish kisses on the pane.

She laughed. It felt good. Fears and worries receded.

Rattling the window, he shouted, "Come out and play with us!" He smacked a kiss on his palm, then held it to the glass.

She briefly covered it with her own. She'd go out to play and store up a few more memories to keep her warm when it grew cold. For now, she wouldn't think beyond today. She'd simply accept the fact that he was the man who made her laugh, haunted her house and dreams, and behind closed doors touched her with unbearable tenderness.

Eight

The school bell rang. Matt walked out of the building with a horde of children. His job at Brownstone Elementary complete, he felt tired, but very good. He was looking forward to concentrating solely on the chamber of commerce film. Too bad Susan was tied up with some church committee meeting that night. His head was bursting with new ideas for the promotional video, and he wanted to share them with her. But that would have to wait until the following night.

He heard Nikki's voice. Glancing over the crowd he located her, then frowned. She appeared to be involved in a shouting match with a boy dressed in tough-guy clothes and wrist chains.

"Shut up, Juicy Fruit!" she yelled.

"Who's gonna make me? You?" the boy jeered.

Me, Matt thought. His protective instincts stood at attention, along with the hair on his neck.

Nikki's expression changed from anger to drop-dead boredom. "Not hardly," she shot back stonily. "You're a dork-brained dweeb. And I really don't care what you say." Tossing her braid over her shoulder, she flounced away.

The juvenile-delinquent-in-training aimed a single-digit salute at Nikki's back. Several reactions and thoughts ran through Matt's mind. Anger—grab the little jerk and rattle his wrist chains. Pride—Nikki had held her own with the bully. Pity—the boy was on the road to trouble in a big way. Matt was saved from having to take action by one of the teachers on bus duty. She collared Juicy Fruit and marched the miscreant back into the school.

Matt went to look for Nikki. He found her sitting alone beneath a tree. Head down, gaze locked on the ground, she didn't acknowledge his presence. She plucked at the grass, sifting broken blades through her fingers. He parked himself and his video equipment beside her.

"Hi, Nik, what's happening?" No response. "Rough day at school?"

"No." She looked up and away.

The thin, tight line of her mouth, the vulnerable look in her half-shuttered eyes, tugged at his heart. Whatever was wrong, he wanted to make it better. "Did that kid upset you?"

She shrugged. "Nope. He's a real pain. He says he likes me, if you can believe that." She rolled her eyes. "I don't pay any attention to him."

He smiled. "I believe it. Boys his age don't know how to talk to girls. So they do silly things, tease and show off. Next week he'll probably like somebody else and leave you alone."

"I know that."

"I feel that you're upset about something. Want to talk about it."

Tears welled up in her eyes. She caught her trembling lower lip between her teeth. "No. I hate to cry in front of people. It's so embarrassing." Her shoulders slumped as though weighed down by a heavy burden. "Thank you," she mumbled, accepting the handkerchief he gave her. She blew her nose loudly.

Matt leaned back against the tree. "We're friends,

right?" She nodded. "Friends help each other. Your friendship is very important to me. You can tell me anything and I'll listen. Maybe I'll understand what you're going through, maybe I won't. But I'll always be your friend and try to help you if it's within my power to do so."

Nikki looked at him. "Tomorrow is Doughnuts for Dad day." Misery clung to her voice like the tears glistening on her eyelashes. "And I don't have a dad. Well I do, but I don't. All I have is a picture of someone who's supposed to be my father."

"Even though he can't be with you, I'm sure he loves you." It hurt a lot to defend the man, but Matt knew it was the right thing to do.

"No, he doesn't." Nikki's eyes flashed with anger. "I haven't seen him in years! He never writes or calls. He doesn't even remember my birthday. Somebody who never says I love you isn't a real father and doesn't count at all. As far as I'm concerned, the only family I've got is Mom and Dellie." She swiped at a fat tear.

Matt gazed helplessly at her. She was breaking his heart. "You're lucky. Your mom and Dellie make a pretty terrific family."

"Yeah," she agreed with a watery smile. "But they can't be dads when I need one. I hate Doughnuts for Dad Day. I'm not the only divorced kid in my class. But I'm the only one who doesn't have a grandfather, or uncle, or brother who can come to breakfast with them. My friends feel sorry for me and the dorkheads tease me about it. Last year I pretended I was sick and Mom let me stay home. I don't think I can get away with it again this year. I'm too healthy. Mom wouldn't buy it."

"Have you told your mother how you feel about this? I'm sure she would understand. She'd be glad to come with you."

"But it just wouldn't be the same. I haven't told her because I don't want to make her feel bad." Her face brightened. "I could invite a guest," she said more to herself than him. "You could be my guest." She turned to him. "Please, Matt, please say you will. It wouldn't take up much of your time. Just an hour. The doughnuts are good. They have jelly doughnuts and chocolate ones too. Please, say you will!"

Seeing the hope radiating from her eyes, Matt knew only a heart chiseled from stone could resist her. He recalled how important it had been to his sister not to feel different and left out. All during Cara's youth he'd attended countless school functions with her. Without hesitation he said, "I'd be honored to be your guest."

The next afternoon Susan took a break from work and joined her family in the kitchen for a snack. She smiled at her daughter. "You look happy today, Nik. Something nice happen at school?"

"It was the best day ever!" Nikki scooped Teddy Bear off the floor and into her arms. "Hi, sweetie. Did you miss me today? I missed you." She kissed him on the nose.

Susan grimaced. "You shouldn't play with the dog at the table." Two pairs of defensive blue-gray eyes turned on her. "Well, you shouldn't."

"Don't you want to know about my day?" Nikki demanded.

Susan's eyes lit up. "You got an A on your math test?"

"There's more to life than getting A's in math, Mom. I didn't get an A."

"Oh, well, I know you tried your best." Susan took a sip of coffee to hide her disappointment. "How did you do?"

"I got," Nikki mumbled, then finished with a shout, "an A plus!"

"That's wonderful, kiddo! I'm so proud of you." Susan looked at Dellie. "Is this a brilliant child, or what?"

"Of course she's brilliant. Takes after her mother," Dellie said. "I knew she could do it."

Nikki beamed. "Just call me Ms. Math Genius. The test was sooo easy, Mom. Matt was right. All I had to do was relax and *see* each problem in my mind as I worked it out."

Mixed emotions surged through Susan. She knew she should be glad Matt had helped Nikki overcome her mental block in math. She *was* happy about it. Delighted. So why was she feeling a bit resentful? Because he'd succeeded where she failed? She masked her inner turmoil with deceptive calmness. "That's great, Nikki. I'm sure Matt will be very excited for you. Don't touch every cookie on the plate after handling that dog."

"He's clean." Nikki selected the fattest chocolate chip cookie. "That wasn't the best part about today, though. Guess what? Matt came to school for the Doughnuts for Dad breakfast. He was my guest! I usually hate that stupid event."

Her cup stilled halfway to Susan's lips. She felt frozen as her daughter's words hit home.

"We had the best time," Nikki went on. "It was so much fun having him for my dad this morning." She giggled. "He gave me a rose. A pink one. Matt ate more doughnuts than Billie Jo's father. Nobody else's dad gave them flowers. We sat with Jenni Shelton and her dad, and Michelle . . ."

Susan swam up through a haze of feelings. She lowered the cup to the table. "He did what?" Her face paled. Sounds became muted and sharp at the same time.

"Mom, haven't you been listening? I said Matt was my dad for the day. I sure wish you'd marry him so he could go with me every year. Dellie, can we have hamburgers for dinner?"

Susan stopped listening. She could barely breathe. *My dad.* A cold, sick feeling settled upon her. He'd played daddy for her child. Hurt and anger fused together. How could he do such a thing without asking her? Give him a little encouragement and he takes over her life and her child! She should have heeded her first instinct about Matt. Inside the charming man was an irresponsible boy.

She'd let him get away with giving Nikki a dog. But acting as surrogate father to her daughter without her consent was too much. *Damn* him. He'd ruined everything. She'd warned him about the fishbowl town. When people knew what he'd done, they would consider it one step away from a wedding announcement! She refused to be railroaded into something she didn't want.

"That man!" Susan stood up so rapidly, her chair wavered, then crashed to the floor. The noise made the puppy jump a few inches off Nikki's lap. Her family was shocked into silence.

Trembling with rage, Susan grabbed her purse and car keys from the counter. "I can't believe he'd do something so stupid. Of all the irresponsible— When I get my hands on that man, I'll strangle him!"

"Mom?"

"Susan dear, are you all right?"

"No, I'm not all right. I'm angry. Matt had no right to play daddy behind my back." Her daughter and aunt stared at her in confusion. She shook her head. They didn't understand how serious this was.

Nikki's eyes filled with tears. "But Mom, Matt's your boyfriend. I thought it would be okay for him to be my guest."

Susan's breath burned in her throat. "I'm sorry, Nikki, but it wasn't okay. I'm not mad at you. Matt should have talked to me first and asked permission."

"Now, Susan dear," Dellie began, "don't you think you're overreacting—"

"No! I cannot condone his irresponsible behavior."

Nikki put the puppy on the floor. Tears streamed down her face. She ran to her mother and threw her arms around her waist. "It's my fault. Please don't be mad at him. Matt was just being my friend. I'm sorry, Mom. I won't do it again. Don't be mad at him."

Susan felt as if her heart were being ripped in two. How could she have been so stupid to allow this to happen? She'd as good as set them all up for heartbreak.

She looked at her great-aunt and gestured helplessly. "Come take Nikki. Please." She ached with the effort to keep the pain away.

"Nooo, Mom! Don't go."

Dellie pried Nikki away and held her close. "Darling girl, don't do anything foolish," she said softly to Susan. "People say things they don't mean when they're angry. Terrible things they can't ever take back. Wait until—"

Not wanting to hear another word, Susan turned and ran out the back door. Nothing was going to prevent her from doing the right thing.

Matt sat back on his heels, wiped his dirty hands on his jeans, and surveyed his handiwork. He'd managed to clear years of neglect out of his backyard. Backbreaking work, but he'd enjoyed every minute of it, embracing the satisfaction and peace that came with working his own small bit of land. With each seed he'd sown in the ground that week, he'd felt himself putting down his own roots. His garden was new. He was new. They'd both grow well in this rich place.

Mentally picturing the way he wanted his yard to look, he stood up and gathered his gardening tools. A bird feeder. It might be pleasant to watch the birds from the kitchen window. He walked into the garage and stored the tools. Yes, sir, he'd buy a bird feeder for his garden. Hell, maybe he'd *build* one. Matt laughed out loud. He'd never built anything in his life, but why let that stand in his way? He'd never planted flowers before either. And he wasn't doing so bad. Mentally adding a book on carpentry to the next day's purchases, he let himself into the house. He needed a shower badly.

Singing, "I stink, therefore, I am," he headed for the bathroom, stripped off his clothes, and stepped into the tub.

When Matt failed to answer the doorbell, Susan walked around to the back and entered the kitchen. She heard the sound of running water and recognized his off-key voice belting out a lusty rendition of an old Beatles' song.

Not bothering to announce her presence, she marched into the bathroom. Grabbing a fistful of shower curtain, she snatched it back. She caught him in the middle of the chorus to "Yellow Submarine."

Matt's gasp ricocheted in the small chamber like a bullet. His arms flapped backward. His feet tried to go in two different directions. The bar of soap he'd been using for a microphone became airborne, sailing past Susan and landing with a thud behind her.

"Holy Mother Malone!" he shouted. He clutched his chest and steadied himself against the tile wall. "What the hell are you doing? Recreating the shower scene from *Psycho*? You scared the bejesus out of me."

"Too bad you didn't break a leg, you weasel." The impact of his nude body along with the steam and spray of water slammed into Susan. She stepped back, distancing herself emotionally as well as physically. Pulling a towel off the rack, she tossed it to him. "Get dressed. We have to talk." The full skirt of her yellow shirtwaist dress swirled around her legs as she turned to stalk out. She slammed the door behind her.

For a moment, Matt stood there, water flowing over him, soaking the towel, splashing onto the floor. Something was very wrong. Swallowing the lump forming in his throat, he threw the wet towel down, turned the faucets off, and stepped out of the tub. He quickly donned a thick navy robe.

Matt opened the door and strode into the bedroom. She wasn't there. He found her in the living room. She reminded him of a caged tiger, pacing back and forth over the Oriental carpet in front of the fireplace, agitation and pent-up fury expressed in each graceful movement. She turned and saw him. The withering, reproachful expression in her eyes took him aback.

"How can you be so irresponsible?" Her fine-boned features tightened with anger. "What were you thinking? Oh, excuse me, I keep forgetting. You don't think. Matt Martinelli just goes with the flow. If it feels good, do it. Never mind how your actions affect other people."

Matt's confusion gave way to hurt, then disbelief. She was calling *him* irresponsible? He'd been steeped in responsibility before he'd been old enough to know what the damn word meant. "Susan, I haven't a shred of an idea what you're talking about."

She glared at him. "I'll bet. You know I'm talking about your playing surrogate father to my daughter. Without my knowledge. Without my consent. I let you get away with giving Nikki a dog. But you're not getting away with this. Not this time."

"I don't know—" He suddenly understood. "Oh, you mean the school breakfast. Angel, Nikki invited me to be her guest this morning. That's all." He ran a hand through his wet hair. "I used to do the same thing for Cara when she was a kid. It didn't occur to me it would upset you. I'm sorry, but given the circumstances, I'd do it again."

She rounded on him, eyes blazing. "How arrogant. There are no circumstances that would give you the right to do what you did without my permission. And I told you not to call me angel."

He crossed his arms over his chest. "Apparently you don't realize what today meant to Nikki. This event is a painful experience for her, one she goes through alone every year. Yesterday—"

"She doesn't have to go through it alone! She has me. She doesn't need a man in her life."

"Speak for yourself. You have no right to speak for her. I found Nikki sitting by herself yesterday crying because some kid was giving her a hard time about not having someone to attend Doughnuts for Dad with her. Did you know last year she pretended she was sick and stayed home so she wouldn't have to show up alone? The poor kid hasn't told you how she feels because she doesn't want to hurt your feelings. You've missed the boat on this one, angel. Try looking at it from Nikki's point of view, not your own."

The implication that she'd consistently overlooked a situation that hurt Nikki struck Susan like a fist. "Don't you dare suggest I neglect my child." She rapidly closed the distance between them. "Nikki adores you. I think you're just using her to railroad me."

"Cool down. You're blowing this thing way out of proportion. Angel, I'm not trying to railroad you into anything." He gently stroked her cheek.

She twisted away. "That's a lie. You've been chasing me all over town since the day we met. You planned this little stunt, knowing people would hear about it and expect us to get married. Even Nikki suggested it. Just put a shotgun to my head and drag me to the church, why don't you?"

"Do you really think I'm so devious?" he asked incredulously.

"You're a genius at it. But you're not getting away with it anymore. Good sex doesn't give you the right to interfere in my life or make false assumptions about our relationship!"

She couldn't have hurt him more if she'd stuck a knife in his chest. Cold fury, unlike anything he'd ever known, exploded inside him. The instinct to strike back curled like a poisonous snake. In a lightning-fast motion, he reached out. His hands clamped on her arms, and he dragged her against him.

"You want to talk about false assumptions? You're full of 'em, lady. You assume I'm trying to trap you. You assume I'm a bum because I don't measure up on your ambition scale. You assume I'd use Nikki to get to you. How can you compartmentalize *me,* what we have together, into a neat little box marked Saturday Night?" He trembled with the need to shake her until she cried for mercy. He wanted to share the pain she'd inflicted upon him. His eyes blazed down into hers. "I'm not your stud service."

Susan blanched. His fingers tightened like steel bands on the soft flesh of her upper arms. Flinching, she tried to break free.

Matt saw fear widen her eyes. He released her so abruptly, she stumbled backward, almost falling. Shock replaced his fury.

He'd wanted to hit her. The realization sickened him. He'd never experienced the urge to strike out physically at someone he loved. Until this moment, the secret fear that he might be like his father hadn't been challenged. Slowly the tension in his body receded. He'd just faced his greatest demon and won. Victory tasted bittersweet.

Feeling older than his years, Matt sat down in the nearest chair. Susan stood motionless in the middle of the room, looking like a wounded butterfly, afraid to flex her tattered wings and fly away. He grieved for her. For himself.

Susan lowered her gaze, unable to face the misery in his eyes. Every ounce of compassion she possessed screamed at her to apologize. Comfort. Ease the horror and torment she'd witnessed in his face. She fought to control her swirling emotions. She couldn't weaken. She had to end it now. Do the right thing for herself and Nikki. "I think it would be best if you left us alone. I don't want to see you anymore."

He rubbed a hand over his face. "I think we both know this isn't about Nikki."

"Of course it is."

He shook his head. "No. It's about you and me. I'm getting too close. That scares the hell out of you, doesn't it? It scares you because you don't trust what we have. That's really the bottom line, trust. Who don't you trust? Me or yourself?"

She refused to meet his gaze. "That's ridiculous. I simply made a mistake in getting involved with you. You're not the right man for me. I knew from the beginning it wasn't going to work." *Why did that feel so painful to say?*

Matt's mouth twisted into a humorless grin. All this time he'd been planning a future for the two of them. And she'd been planning to say good-bye. "Not the right man. Not the button-down, ambitious type is what you mean. I won't apologize for how I make a living. I enjoy running a video store and making films. You're using your ideal image of success—and Nikki—as excuses. Why are you so afraid of making a commitment with any man?"

She glared at him. "I'm not afraid! I did make a commitment once. All I got in return was heartache."

"Sometimes that happens. We all get heartaches." His was aching like hell at the moment. "It's called taking a risk on life. But you're too hung up on the past to take that risk, aren't you? Before we met, you chose the men you went out with. Nice, safe buddies. But I'm different. I chose you. I approached first and you can't handle it."

They stared at each other. The silence grew, seeming to fill the room like liquid. Susan felt as if she were drowning in it. She had to escape. "I don't have to listen to such nonsense." She spun away, almost running in her panic.

She got as far as the door before he spoke again. "You're the best thing that's ever happened to me. I love you."

Raw emotion welled up in her throat. "Don't say that."

"I'm crazy about you and Nikki. You're beautiful, bright, and caring. And I do love you. If you don't care for me, nothing I can say or do will make any difference. I won't try to change your mind. I won't chase after you anymore. But do yourself a favor. If you can't love me . . . love somebody. Let the past go. Don't do it for Nikki. Don't do it for me. Do it for yourself."

Her legs didn't want to hold her upright. She held on to the doorknob. She didn't want to believe him. It was only an attempt to sway her emotions. He'd say anything to keep her from walking out the door. *Don't say you love me*, she wanted to scream at him. "Just leave us alone, Matt."

"I promised Nikki my friendship. That has nothing to do with whether you and I are lovers or enemies. It will hurt her if I renege on my promise."

"She'll get over it."

"For her sake, I hope you're right."

"We don't need you."

Matt watched her leave. She closed the door softly behind her without a backward glance. His gaze flickered around the living room he'd once thought warm and cozy. It suddenly seemed cold and empty.

Nine

Over the next few days Matt concentrated on getting through each one, five minutes at a time. The grapevine was burning with gossip. People he barely knew felt free to offer him helpful hints to repair the break with Susan.

Fred the florist was convinced the way to a woman's heart was flowers. He offered Matt a wholesale discount.

Old Bill Walker advised him to go off bass fishing for a few days, the idea being that absence makes a woman's heart grow fonder. The devout fisherman was appalled when Matt confessed his experience with fish was limited to trout amandine served by a waiter.

Reesa and Scott advised him to camp out on Susan's porch until she agreed to discuss the incident rationally.

Myrtle Cooper and three luncheonette clients counseled him to beg Susan's forgiveness, whether he was in the wrong or not. A gentleman in bib overalls, eavesdropping from a nearby table, violently objected to the plan. He claimed the only way to get a woman over a snit was to make her jealous. Matt paid his bill and left when a battle-of-the-sexes argument broke out.

While Matt was filling in for a sick employee at the video store, a group of teenage girls came in. After a whispered conference, one girl with her hair in dreadlocks and braces on her teeth broke away from the rest and approached the counter. She told him they'd been thinking about his problem with Ms. Wright. The group's consensus was that he should kidnap her and take her on a romantic cruise to the Bahamas.

Only the gravity of his situation tempted his inclination to lock himself in a room and laugh until he cried. It was truly ironic that he'd been so completely accepted by the folks of Millers Creek and rejected by the one person who counted most.

Friday night Susan lay in bed, trying to massage away a headache. It was working as well as her efforts to forget about Matt. She hadn't seen him for several days, then that morning she'd run into him on the street. They'd spoken politely, both awkwardly ignoring their total awareness of the other. Every screaming beat of her heart had urged her to throw herself in his arms. She'd walked away with her emotions bleeding from every pore.

She threw back the bed linens and got up. It was a cool spring night, but she didn't bother to cover her feverish skin with a robe. She walked into the bathroom and took a couple of aspirin. Waiting for the pain relievers to kick in, she stood at the window. The moon dominated the black sky. It was a lover's moon, full of promise and overbright.

"It wasn't meant to be," she whispered. She had nothing in common with Matt. She wanted more out of life. He was happy with what he had. She worked hard at her business. He worked hard at playing. She was a realist. He was a dreamer. Their being together made no sense. So why did she feel like the world's biggest heel? An opinion, she thought wryly, shared by her family, friends, and the mailman.

The house was too quiet, inviting reflection. She wandered out into the hall, then continued on to Nikki's room. Moonlight streamed in through the lace curtains, haloing her daughter's still form.

Susan thought about the mood at home. It was grim. Nikki wasn't speaking to her. The look of constant rebuke in the child's eyes was killing her. At least Dellie wasn't openly boycotting her too. But her aunt was behaving unusually preoccupied as she went around putting shoes in the refrigerator, salt in the sugar bowl.

Susan drifted toward the bed. Teddy Bear lifted his silky head and gazed up at her in his funny, myopic way. She sat on the edge of the bed and reached out to brush tresses away from Nikki's face.

She'd always believed Nikki couldn't miss something she'd never had. Brian hadn't been home much when they were married. Nikki wasn't suffering from the lack of a father figure. Was she?

The feeling that Matt had spoken the truth nagged at her. Had she been blind to her child's need? Had she been so wrapped up in protecting herself, that she'd readily seized upon any excuse to break off a relationship that demanded an emotional commitment?

"I'm sorry, baby," she whispered. "I've made a terrible mess of everything." Feeling sick at heart, she went back to her own room.

The art supplies Matt had given her caught her eye. She'd left them stacked on a table, untouched and forgotten. She switched on a lamp. Her fingers trembled as she picked up a sketch pad. Sinking down into a chair, she reached for a box of pastels. She chose a stick of color, held it experimentally in her hand. It felt strange, but soothingly familiar.

Susan positioned the pastel over the paper. Her

fingers seemed to know what to do even if her mind didn't. She stroked shape and color onto the page. Time passed. She didn't notice.

Stopping as abruptly as she'd started, she looked at what she'd done. Her eyes widened with slight shock. Where had this come from? she wondered in awe.

She'd captured the scene from the garden—Matt caught in the act of swinging Nikki off her feet; Teddy Bear racing excitedly around Matt's legs; Dellie and Billie Jo looking on.

The inner vision she'd lacked in her youth leapt off the page, vibrating with life. Her style was softer, deceptively simple, relying on emotion and maturity instead of intricate, hard-edged details and deliberate format. The joy of the moment shone in her daughter's laughing face.

And Matt. His expressive eyes blazed up at the child with humor as well as something she'd failed to recognize when she'd stood watching them.

Love. Warm, affectionate, unselfish love. Her subconscious had registered what she'd failed to notice.

Susan held the sketch pad tightly. Slowly, she understood that the work not only portrayed love, it had been created with love bursting to find an outlet.

She lowered the sketch to her lap. Her mind began to clear, and she felt calm and connected. At last she allowed herself to acknowledge she loved Matt Martinelli.

The first rays of dawn crept into the room. Susan remained by the window, savoring her newfound sense of freedom and peace.

"I can't stand it any longer," Dellie said, storming into the kitchen the next morning. "This has gone on long enough. I can't bear to see you make the same mistakes I made. I didn't raise you to be an emotional coward like me. You apologize to that wonderful young man and let me get some sleep!"

Startled, Susan looked up from her coffee. "Dellie, you aren't making any sense. What mistakes? I don't understand."

"Well, of course not. I never told you about Harry."

"Harry who?"

"My Harry. The young man I wanted to marry." She opened a cabinet, then slammed it shut. "Who moved the tea tin?"

"You did. It's in the toaster oven. I didn't know you had ever been in love."

Dellie found the tea. "I fell in love when I was seventeen. But Papa didn't approve of my young man. Harry wanted to elope. I was appalled by the thought of running away. Too frightened to leave my family and everything so familiar. We had an awful row and said terrible things to each other. Harry left town and I never saw him again."

Susan walked over to her aunt. "Oh, Dellie. I'm so sorry. How hurt you must have been."

Dellie met Susan's gaze, her eyes serious. "It broke my heart. Just like you, I vowed no one would ever get close enough to break my heart again. Don't fall into the same trap I did, darling girl. Forgive Matt. He really didn't do anything so dreadful. He loves you and Nikki very much."

Susan smiled and laid a hand on top of Dellie's. "I know."

Her aunt gave her a puzzled look. "You do?"

"I love him too."

"Well, it's about time. Don't just stand there, go get dressed. Matt's going to videotape the children at Camp Pine Ridge today. Good heavens, where did I put that book on wildflowers?"

Saturday morning Matt guided the Jag out of Millers Creek. It was a perfect day for being outdoors—sunny and warm with just a hint of a breeze rustling through the trees. He darted a glance at his watch. He was running late. No big surprise, considering his lack of sleep lately. The scouting events at Camp Pine Ridge would already be under way.

Susan would be there. Matt swore silently. He wanted her back in his life. He'd struggled to make polite small talk with her when he'd seen her the previous day. Crazy thoughts had kept getting in the way. He'd wanted to touch her, kiss her. Hold on to her until neither of them could think of letting go.

He couldn't take much more. Sometimes he felt as if he were one step away from crossing the line of acceptable behavior. The kidnapping idea was beginning to sound good. Was he nuts or what?

A whole day of being near her might stretch his good sense to the limits. Good thing they'd be chaperoned by seventy-five ten-to twelve-year-old girls and a couple of dozen scout leaders and parents. Otherwise, he didn't think any court in the nation would hold him responsible for his actions.

He turned off the two-lane highway onto a narrow dirt road. Balloons and streamers hung from shrubs and trees, along with a banner welcoming camp day patrons. The Jag bounced over the rutted lane. He prayed the shocks wouldn't die in horror from such rough treatment.

Finally, he reached the campsite and parked beside a small wooden building in the center of a grassy knoll. Tents and crudely built outhouses nestled in a grove of oaks and maples off to the right. He gathered his video equipment and got out. A blur of shorts-clad children ran giggling past him.

Another set of gigglers told him where to find the event's coordinator. Matt spoke with her for a few minutes, filmed her group as they practiced first aid on each other, then went in search of Susan.

He found her sitting cross-legged by a campfire, giving the kids surrounding her a lesson on fire safety. Just looking at her filled him with an emotion too much for one man to endure. She could pass for a teenager with her hair braided in a single plait like Nikki's. She wore denim shorts and an emerald-green polo shirt. He particularly liked the way the shorts molded her perfectly shaped fanny and showed off her long legs. He backed off and began filming, using a maple tree for cover.

Susan noticed the girls were getting restless. They were probably bored with safety rules, she figured and wanted to get to the good stuff. She wound up her talk, then helped the kids as they marked off each individual cooking area with a circle of stones.

"Okay," she called out, "take out your supplies and let's start cooking." She got to her feet and stretched.

"Ms. Wright, there's a man with a camera behind that tree."

Susan's gaze followed the child's pointing finger. *Matt!* Her pulse began pounding, as if she'd just run a marathon. He lowered the camcorder, and for a moment they stood motionless, staring at each other.

His hair shone like black glass in the sunlight. Susan wished she could see his eyes, but they were hidden by his sunglasses. She loved him. Loved him, worn jeans, red and aqua high-top sneakers, and all. And he didn't even know it.

Feeling as awkward as a schoolboy, Matt couldn't stop looking at her. Every breath he drew seemed charged with pure energy. To his pleasure, he saw a blush stain her face a dusky rose. Her mouth curved into a smile so dazzling, it almost brought him to his knees.

A light tap on his shoulder broke the spell. "Mr. Martinelli, my troop is ready for you now."

He murmured "fine" to the scout leader claiming his attention. Reluctantly, he gathered his equipment case and followed the woman.

Susan watched him walk away, taking her heart with him. It was torture knowing he was so near and not being able to tell him she loved him. Her brow wrinkled in frustration, and she turned to supervise the cooking preparations.

A few minutes later she saw Matt again. He was heading toward the woods with a set of high-spirited little imps and their leader, Dottie. He had them singing "Yellow Submarine" at the top of their very healthy lungs.

Susan wondered if anyone had bothered to warn him that Dottie's troop was notorious for their pranks. Grinning, she began to hum the same Beatles' tune.

Soon another woman came to take over Susan's duties. Susan grabbed a diet cola from a cooler and stationed herself where she could see Matt the minute he returned from his hike. An attack of nerves assailed her as she planned the things she would say to him.

Before long, Dottie emerged from the woods with one of her girls.

Susan went to meet them. "What happened?"

Dottie rolled her eyes. "Missy sat in poison ivy. Do me a favor and go check on the rest of my hellions, would you. They're practicing tying knots down by the rope bridge."

"Okay. Is Matt still with them?"

"Uh-huh. Rescue the poor man before they push him in the river or something." Dottie herded her stiff-legged charge toward the first-aid station.

On the wooded trail leading to the river, Susan ran into the rest of Dottie's troop. They stopped laughing when they saw her. Their expressions became driven-snow pure.

"Where's Mr. Martinelli?" she asked.

"Back there," one said with a giggle.

"Is he alive?"

The girls screamed with laughter and started to run.

Suspecting foul play, Susan hurried on to investigate.

• • •

"Aw, come on, girls, you've had your laugh. Girls? There's a fly tap-dancing on my nose. It's as big as a horse. Holymothermurphy. *Helllpppp!* Somebody-anybody."

Susan followed the downhill path toward the sound of Matt's voice. Soon the tangle of trees gave way to undergrowth. As she neared the riverbank she came to a clearing of dense grass. Shading her eyes with a hand, she stopped and scanned the area. She spied the rope bridge stretching over the water, and a couple of yards away, she located him. She stared in disbelief . . .

He was sitting on the ground . . .

legs stretched out . . .

arms pinned to his sides . . .

tied to a tree.

Laughter bubbled up in her throat. He'd been had by Dottie's hellions!

Matt's head swiveled around, then he grinned with relief. "Susan! Am I glad to see you. A bear almost attacked me. Get me out of here."

"Relax, city man. There are no bears in these woods."

"Okay, let's not quibble. Maybe it was a squirrel. But it was a big one. It looked at me with beady, hungry eyes."

She sauntered toward him, betraying her desire to rush. Matt's grin faded a bit. Silently, he watched her perch daintily on a stump. She cupped her chin in her palm and subjected him to a thoughtful stare.

All sorts of possibilities occurred to Susan as she gazed at him. The wariness in his heavenly brown eyes upped her good humor a notch. She smiled slowly. "Perhaps I should come back later when you aren't so tied up."

"You're enjoying my plight. That's really heartless. Did I mention these ropes are getting tight?"

"Looks like you have a rather knotty problem."

He groaned and looked toward the sky. "I'm dying here and she turns into a comedian."

She grinned. "I love a captive audience. Want me to *leaf* you alone?"

"That's worse than my orange pun." She seemed totally at ease with him, he realized. The ice was broken. His spirits soared.

"How did you get roped into this situation?" she asked.

"They wanted to demonstrate their proficiency with square knots."

"And you fell—ah, sat for it?"

"They seemed like such sweet kids. You are going to untie me, aren't you?" He gave her his sale-of-the-century smile.

"Poor Jaguar man." Susan rose. "Victimized by a bunch of sweet little girls." She walked over to him and straddled his legs, then gracefully sank to her knees in a smooth motion. The flash of surprise in his eyes afforded her a measure of satisfaction.

"Something tells me I'm about to victimized by a big girl," he murmured. At least, he hoped and prayed he was. The intimate affection in her smile zeroed in on his senses like a heat-seeking missile. "Uh, 'Jaguar man'?"

She let her fingers do the walking up his chest. "That's how I think of you sometimes." She removed the Ray-Bans stowed in his shirt pocket and settled them on the tip of his nose.

He peered at her over the rim of the glasses. "Makes me sound like a predator."

She traced the curve of his jaw, delighting in the flare of longing in his eyes. "Aren't you?" She lowered herself onto his lap.

He was very conscious of her firm bottom pressing against his thighs. It had a startlingly arousing effect on him. He wanted to pull her close and cover her mouth with his own. What a hell of a time to be tied to a tree. "Some predator," he said derisively. "I feel more like a trussed-up Thanksgiving turkey."

She laughed softly, her breath feathering his face. When she wiggled, she felt his immediate reaction. "Oh, my, what do we have here? You're temperature's rising, sir."

Totally enchanted, he murmured, "I'd say my temperature is going through the roof—so to speak. Here we are, alone in the woods. Me tied to a tree. Helpless. You could do anything you want to me and there'd be no one to hear my cries for help."

"Do you want help?"

"Good lord, no! This is a little kinky, but I love it." It was the stuff his dreams were made of. The only problem was he wanted to touch her in return. Frustration furrowed his brow, and he squirmed against his bonds.

"Something wrong?" she cooed.

He grinned. "Untie me and find out."

"Maybe I will." Her voice dropped to a husky whisper. "And maybe I won't." She laid her hand on his chest. "I can feel your heartbeat."

"Beating like hell, I imagine." Her mouth was just a kiss away, driving him crazy.

"Uh-huh." She shifted the sunglasses to the top of his head.

Matt held perfectly still as she inched closer. He felt riveted by her smoky gaze. Anticipation became an exquisite torture. If he could live two lifetimes, he'd never get enough of her touching him.

Leaning closer still, Susan smiled against his lips. She kissed him lightly once, twice. Her arms wound around his neck. Her lips parted, welcoming an urgent kiss. She felt as if she'd come home after a long and lonely absence.

It no longer mattered that they were poles apart in ambition. She didn't care that he marched to his own tune, played by his own laid-back rules. He was loving and generous. That was all she needed to know.

She tipped her head back, allowing his mouth to caress her throat. Waves of pleasure radiated deep in the core of her femininity, where his arousal pressed against her. She could feel her body tremble with the power of her response.

Completely caught up in her love for him, she captured his face between her hands. "I'm sorry," she whispered, resting her forehead against his. "So sorry. I love you. Love you. I didn't mean any of the terrible things I said. You were right. I was afraid. But not anymore. I do love you. Forgive me. I—"

"Angel, there's only one way to shut you up." Matt hungrily pressed his mouth to hers.

They broke apart, breathing rapidly.

"Shut me up again," she demanded.

He readily complied.

Coming up for air, Matt suddenly remembered something important. "Ah, angel mine, I believe we've just shot the hell out of today's G rating."

"What?"

"The camera's running." He inclined his head to the right.

For the first time Susan noticed his camcorder propped up on a fallen tree, aimed directly at them. Her face turned Technicolor red. "Oh my God!" She practically jumped off his lap.

"Ever made love on a riverbank?" he asked.

Ten

It was well after midnight when Matt gradually awakened. A steady rain beat against his bedroom window. He rolled over, nestling closer to Susan. He kissed her bare shoulder. She murmured his name in her sleep, instinctively fitting herself into the curve of his body.

An odd disquiet that had nothing to do with the rain ruled his spirits. He traced the line from her hip to her satin thigh, loving the feel of her skin.

She had come home with him from Camp Pine Ridge. He'd plied her with pasta. They'd laughed and danced after dinner in the kitchen, then made love for hours before drifting into satisfied slumber.

His hands traveled back to rest upon the gentle dip of her waist. Now she was where she belonged. Beside him.

Wariness crept into his unsettled mood. But for how long? he couldn't help wondering. How long?

He realized he'd been so caught up in having her with him again, in healing the rift between them, that not one word had been spoken about their future. He lay on his back and stared at the ceiling. She'd taken the initiative that day and had said she loved him. He believed her. He'd felt the love in their passion. He'd known enough passion without love to recognize the difference.

That she loved him he didn't doubt. Where she wanted their relationship to go was another matter. He didn't have a clue. Were they back to square one? A grim expression tightened his features. He couldn't return to the way things were. He wanted more than Saturday nights.

He glanced at her. She looked so sweet and peaceful. He hated to wake her, but he'd reached a turning point. Unable to go backward, he could only go forward. It was time she knew certain things about him, things that might alter the course of their future. And he needed to know what she wanted, how she envisioned him in her life.

He slid his arm around her waist and stroked the smooth plane of her stomach. She sighed softly, snuggling against him. He woke her slowly, blazing a string of kisses along her neck and cheek. She responded by turning toward him. Her eyelashes fluttered open. He rose up on his elbow and looked down into her smoky eyes. "Hello, angel."

Susan smiled sleepily. " 'Lo. Have you been awake long?"

"Awhile. I've been thinking about us."

The serious tone in his voice chased away all remnants of sleep. Fully alert, she returned his intense gaze. "Is something wrong?"

"No. I hope not. I need to tell you how I feel."

She reached up to caress his face. "You told me. Many times, as I well remember."

He captured her hand, kissed her palm. "You make me feel so happy and whole. I need you." Her brilliant smile fed the volatile hunger pouring through his veins. "I need to be more than part of your Saturday night routine. I want to wake up every morning and know I'll find you beside me. I'd like us to share a life together, loving and supporting each other through the bad days as well as the good. When the going gets rough, I want us to be able to yell, let off steam, and know one of us isn't going to run out the door."

He paused for a second, noting her subtle shifting away from him. Her defensive gesture appeared to be an unconscious one, but it saddened him. Making everything right for both of them could very well prove his greatest challenge. Or worst nightmare. Either way, it was only fair for her to know where he stood.

He smiled faintly. "I realize you probably feel I'm pushing too fast. But our relationship is very important to me. I need to know if you're as committed as I am."

She eased herself into a sitting position, pulling the sheet around her.

"I want to marry you," he said quietly.

Susan was aware of his stillness, aware of the hard pounding of her heart. She looked away, oddly humbled by the strength of his feelings. Humbled. Exalted. Apprehensive.

In the growing silence she glanced at him, and found him watching her in expectation. Offering a tremulous smile, she stroked his hair. "I love you too. You've altered my perception of my life. I don't know how it happened, but you've changed me inside against my will. You've shown me what I've been missing and just how dull my life had become. This past week I discovered how I felt being apart from you. I didn't like it. I was miserable. I've barely had time to come to terms with it all. I can promise you I am committed to making our relationship work. But marriage . . ." She wasn't ready to go completely beyond the safety of the barriers she'd built around herself.

She slid down until they were eye level. His expression was stark and searching. She touched his face. "Please try to understand that the thought of marrying again is still a bit overwhelming for me. Will you give me time to think about it?"

Matt kissed her trembling fingers with infinite tenderness. "Of course, angel." He was relieved she wasn't rejecting the idea of marriage outright. Her willingness to consider his proposal gave him the strength to risk opening himself up to her further. He drew her into his arms. "There are other things you should know about me. Before I came to Millers Creek, I—"

"Not now." She cradled his face between her hands. "Just hold me."

"But Susan, it's important that I tell—"

"Please, love, I don't want to talk anymore tonight. There's so little time left before I have to leave for home."

She kissed him persuasively. As a flame to a fuse, she ignited a passion so fierce, it banished his good intentions.

Matt's proposal was on Susan's mind as she entered Walker's luncheonette Wednesday afternoon. Would he expect a definite answer today? She'd asked herself that same question each time she'd been with him over the past three days. Ironically enough, she realized she was the source of the pressure she felt, not Matt. He hadn't mentioned marriage or attempted to influence her in any way.

Glancing around, she noted he hadn't yet arrived for their lunch date. Heading for her usual spot, she smiled and spoke to two of her aunt's friends, then sat down to wait for him.

As she plucked a napkin from its chrome container, she admitted that thinking about marrying again terrified her. She wished she had Matt's unshakable faith that they could make it work. But she was too well acquainted with the little things that could destroy a marriage. And fate had a way of knocking complacency out into left field when least expected. She'd failed so badly once. She simply couldn't bear the thought of failing again.

She started to place the napkin on her lap and realized she'd shredded it to pieces. Blushing, she checked to see if anyone was watching her. Dellie's friends, Rachel and Mary Jane, were staring at her curiously. Painting on a false smile, she stared back until they looked away.

This marriage thing was making her crazy! She scooped up the napkin pieces and stuffed them into an ashtray. Maybe they could compromise on a long engagement. No, she didn't really believe he would go for it. He wanted more. She doubted an engagement would constitute more in his eyes.

Myrtle swam through the crowd and set a glass of iced tea in front of her. "Matt phoned, 'bout an hour ago. Said to tell you something came up, and he can't meet you for lunch. I sure am glad you two got back together."

"Did he say why?"

The waitress shook her head. "He was rushing off somewhere. Said he'd talk to you later." She took Susan's order and left.

Susan was reaching for her briefcase, figuring she'd go over some work during her solitary lunch, when she heard her name.

"Poor Susan. Did you hear that, Mary Jane?"

Susan stiffened. What was Rachel Henderson up to?

"I certainly did," Mary Jane answered. "*He* was supposed to meet Susan for lunch."

Susan rolled her eyes. Sometimes she wished she had the luxury of anonymity, but it was impossible in this small town!

"Of all the nerve," Rachel said with more glee than censure. "If I was the kind of person who butted into other people's business—" The elderly woman paused, then spoke louder, "—I'd give that Italian Romeo a piece of my mind."

Susan barely stifled a gasp. Dellie's so-called friends

meant her to overhear their conversation! If Rachel Henderson gave a piece of her mind, she thought wryly, it wouldn't leave her with much. And the Italian Romeo? she repeated indignantly on Matt's behalf. What had he done to set the bees buzzing in the old biddies' bonnets?

"The man's an utter cad." Delight rang in Mary Jane's wavery voice. "I feel so sorry for Susan. Do you think she knows yet?"

The fine hair on Susan's neck practically stood at attention. Cad? *Her* Matt? Her brows drew together like twin thunderclouds as her hand tightened on the glass of iced tea. What did they think they knew that she didn't?

"Dear me, no," Rachel said. "And *I* certainly wouldn't want to be the one to tell her the bad news."

Bad news? Susan swung around to face the ladies. "Tell her what?" she asked in a frigid tone.

Rachel delicately patted her blue-tinted hair. "Oh, dear, we didn't mean you to hear it from us did we, Mary Jane? But forewarned is forearmed, I always say."

Susan didn't miss the love of gossip and mischief shining in Rachel Henderson's eyes. The next time the old witch pinched Nikki's cheeks, Susan thought, the child had her permission to retaliate with a swift kick to the shins!

"Mary Jane and I were coming out of Nancy's dress shop about twenty minutes ago, and we saw him. He was sitting in that cute little sports car of his at a red light. There was a woman with him. A brunette. Very sophisticated-looking. She's not from around here, I can tell you that."

"Nobody we know," Mary Jane chirped in agreement. "Probably some floozy from Greensboro. She cuddled right up to him in broad daylight on Main Street, for heaven's sake. And she kissed him on the cheek."

Susan's eyes began to burn. What they were insinuating couldn't possibly be true.

Rachel peered at Susan. "He certainly didn't seem to mind. Men are such scoundrels, aren't they, dear?"

Susan couldn't speak, couldn't even catch her breath. Finally, she managed to respond in a tight voice, "So are some *ladies* who have nothing better to do than spread malicious gossip." She turned her back on them.

"Well!" Rachel huffed. "Some people are so ungrateful. Let's go, Mary Jane."

In a distant portion of her mind Susan heard chairs scrape the tile floor, packages rattle, flowered silk dresses softly rustle as the two women made their exit. Then unreasonable panic set in. All her old fears and insecurities surfaced. Tears swam in her vision.

Why believe the worst? a saner voice in her mind questioned. He might have his faults, but she could not believe infidelity was one of them. If she'd learned one thing about him, it was that his sense of loyalty was deeply ingrained.

She drew in a ragged breath. The pale imitation of love she'd felt for Brian was nothing in comparison to what she felt for Matt. He freely gave more than he received. Love without condition.

So who was the woman? An old girlfriend who'd tracked him down from Chicago?

Susan pushed her chair back and stood up.

Matt loved her. He belonged to her. She knew in her heart he wasn't the two-timing type. He clearly needed rescuing. Determination lent her strength. She tossed some money on the table and grabbed her belongings.

No man-stealing floozy from Chicago or outer space was going to try to lure Matt away from her!

Susan marched up to Matt's front door. She pressed the door chime, tapped her foot impatiently, pounded a fist on the door.

She heard someone approaching. The lock clicked, and a brown eye fringed with feathery black lashes to die for peered at her through a crack in the door.

"Yes? May I help you?"

The floozy had Chicago stamped all over her vocal cords, Susan thought as she glared icily into that lone brown eye. "I'm Susan Wright. I want to speak to Matt."

"He went to the grocery store. Would you like to come in and wait for him? He should be back soon."

"Yes, I would. And I think you and I should have a little chat."

The door opened wide, and the woman stepped back into the shadow to let Susan in. "I'd like that. Please come in. Matt's told me so much about you."

Susan walked into the hallway. "Who are—" The words died in her throat as the other woman moved into the light.

Exquisitely beautiful was a paltry description for her Sophia Loren kiss-me lips, exotic cheekbones, and large, extraordinary eyes. The term pocket Venus had been invented for someone like her. She was five one, maybe, with all the generous curves God intended a female to possess. Her child-like size and flawless complexion made it impossible to pin down her age. She could have been anywhere between twenty and thirty. Raven-black hair flowed to her waist, draped seductively over one breast.

And the hussy was wearing Matt's robe!

"I can't tell you how much I appreciate all you've done for Matt," she was saying. "I'm so glad we have this chance to meet."

Susan ignored the hand extended to her. She'd rather eat dirt and die than shake her hand.

Oddly enough, the woman didn't seem offended. Instead, a slow smile spread across her full lips.

Instant recognition took Susan aback. She'd been on the receiving end of such a smile hundreds of times. "Are you related to Matt?" she asked hesitantly.

"He's my brother."

"You're Cara Martinelli?"

Cara's fine dark eyes glittered with laughter. "O'Mally. I married a redheaded Irishman two years ago."

Susan shook her head, unable to hold the woman's gaze. "I'm so embarrassed. You can't imagine what I've been thinking."

"I believe I can. If I discovered a strange woman in my husband's bathrobe, I'd get hostile too. Would you like a cup of coffee?"

"I'd love one."

They walked into the kitchen together.

"How long do you plan to be in town?" Susan asked as she selected her favorite blend of coffee from the several varieties Matt stocked.

"Until tomorrow morning."

"Good heavens! You came all the way from California to visit your brother for one day?"

Cara laughed. "No. I was in New York on a business trip and things wrapped up faster than I'd planned. I had some free time before going on to Atlanta, so I called Matt at the crack of dawn and invited myself down. In all honesty, I wanted to check you out."

Susan smiled ruefully. "My ninja-avenger act didn't make such a great first impression, I'm afraid." She finished preparing the coffee and joined Cara at the table.

"No problem. What I saw was a woman protecting her man. I'm glad you feel so strongly about my brother." She gazed speculatively at Susan. "He's very much in love with you. You're not going to hurt him, I hope."

Tension sizzled between them as the two women stared at each other. The room was as still as a mausoleum at midnight.

Maintaining eye contact, Susan answered simply, "I love Matt."

Apparently the quiet certainty in the way she spoke was all the reassurance Cara needed. Her acceptance was as tangible as her sunny smile.

They swapped pleasantries for a few minutes, then began discussing their respective businesses. Cara astonished Susan by casually mentioning that she would never have been able to finance her graphic arts company without Matt's backing. Half-listening, Susan wondered how he had managed to finance his sister's business as well as the video store on a salesman's salary.

"I'm glad I made this trip," Cara went on. "I've been so worried about Matt. But he's looking healthy, and more relaxed and happy than he's ever been before. It's obvious his new life agrees with him. He's a changed man. I'm talking a one-hundred-eighty de-gree, radical change. The difference in his attitude amazes me. Like night and day."

"Oh, really?" Susan said, bewildered.

"I swear, if you'd seen him when we thought he'd had a heart attack a year ago, you'd understand. What a nightmare! I've never felt so helpless and scared. I was so afraid of losing him. Fortunately, it turned out to be less serious. Arrhythmia is some-thing he can live with, thank God."

For a second Susan just stared at her, then the full force of Cara's words exploded in her head.

Eleven

"Matt's always been my rock," Cara said as Susan gazed blindly at her, mentally reeling from the shock. "He and Rick—my husband—are the two most important people in the world to me. I can't bear the thought of anything happening to either of them."

The trembling began in Susan's shoulders, then swept along her arms. She couldn't retain her grasp on the mug. Gripping it with both hands, she eased it down on the table. Taking a deep breath, she fought for control.

"He seems fine now," she managed to say. *Arrhythmia?* A terrifying pressure built up in her chest.

Cara nodded solemnly. "His doctor told him he had to change his stressful life-style or die. No more eighteen-hour workdays. Resigning his position as vice-president of international sales was the best thing he's ever done for himself." She mentioned the name of Matt's former company. Susan recognized it as one of the most prestigious computer companies in the country. Then Cara went on to recount with distaste how Matt had poured his life and energy into developing its multimillion-dollar contracts. "There was no need for him to drive himself so hard," Cara said. "But there was something inside him that constantly demanded he live up to his ideal of the successful man. I think he used to believe his self-worth was somehow measured by his bank accounts."

More guilt heaped itself upon Susan's growing hysteria. Pain slashed her when she remembered how often she'd thrown his lack of ambition in his face.

"I wish he'd left the company years ago," Cara said. "It's good to see him enjoying life." She laughed. "He loves the video store. Reel to Real is perfect for him. He's so proud of it. I—"

She stopped and stared at Susan's ashen face. "Are you all right?" Comprehension suddenly dawned in her eyes. "You didn't know," she whispered. Reaching for Susan's shaking hands, she held them between her own. "Susan, I'm sorry. I didn't mean to upset you. Matt's fine and will outlive both of us if he continues to take care of himself. Believe me. Arrhythmia is an irregular heartbeat. Left untreated, it can be life-threatening. But he takes medication to control it, watches his diet, and he's reduced the stress in his life. Oh, God, your hands are cold as ice! This is terrible. I feel like I've unwittingly trashed you twice today. Matt is going to cream me for this."

Susan withdrew her hands from Cara's. Closing her eyes, she pressed her fingertips against her temples, as if desperately trying to hold herself together. She'd had more than she could take for one day.

"Forgive me, Susan. I really thought Matt had told you."

The abject misery in Cara's voice got through to her, and induced a measure of sympathy in her. Seeing Cara's concerned expression, Susan sighed and half smiled. "I think he tried to tell me." She thought of the night he had proposed. *There are things you need to know about me,* he'd said. "And I wouldn't let him."

She stood up. Her legs felt wobbly. "I'd better go now."

"Stay," Cara urged, rising. "Matt will be home soon."

Susan shook her head. "I need to be alone for a while. I hope you understand. I'm glad we met. Have a safe trip home." Not giving Cara a chance to say anything more, she quickly walked out of the kitchen.

Matt was stepping onto the front porch, his arms filled with grocery bags, as she rushed out of the house. "Whoa, angel mine! Where are you running off to? I was going to call you later. Could you and Dellie and Nikki come over for dinner tonight?"

Round-eyed, Susan stared at him. She felt suspended between agony and ecstasy. It was all she could do not to place her hand over his heart to ensure herself it was beating strong and true. Reaching up, she gently touched his face and drew his head down for a kiss. His lips parted for her, and she kissed him as if it were their last.

Matt was about to drop the grocery bags and embrace her, when she released him.

"I love you."

Wondering at the catch in her voice and the fragile expression in her eyes, he said softly, "I love you too. What about dinner?"

She backed away. "I don't know." Turning, she hurried toward her car.

Mystified, Matt followed her. "Is something wrong?"

She jerked the car door open. "No!"

His brows came together in a scowl. "Did you meet my sister?"

"Yes." She slammed the door and started the engine.

Matt watched her tear out of the driveway, then, bellowing Cara's name, he stalked back into the house.

•   •   •

The city limits of Millers Creek were behind Susan. Lost in a fog of emotion, she aimlessly followed the two-lane highway. The Camp Pine Ridge sign caught her eye. She veered onto the dirt road leading to the deserted camp.

After parking her car, Susan hiked the trail toward the river. The heels of her pumps sank into the soft earth with each step. Low branches whipped at her skirt and occasionally snagged her panty hose. She paid no attention. Her mind was set only on reaching the last place where anyone would think of looking for her, a quiet place where she could be completely alone.

She came to the area where the girls had practiced their knots on Matt. Feeling suddenly old and tired, she sat down on the ground. For a while all she could do was stare at the river. The muddy water flowed leisurely under the rope bridge, making a soft, lapping sound against the rocks along the embankment.

The emotions and thoughts she'd held in check abruptly tumbled forth like a tidal wave. For years she'd avoided examining her feelings too closely, but now she was forced to confront them. An overwhelming fear of failure had been her driving force for so long. Her fear of emotional intimacy had kept her locked on the course she'd chosen.

Then Matt had entered her life and began picking away at her layers of insulation. Since she'd known him, life had taken on a richer hue. He'd managed to touch that long-frozen part of her, and she'd started to feel again. He'd been the catalyst to the changes within her. She hadn't wanted to love him, but she did.

And she'd looked into the face of the man she loved and had glimpsed his mortality. A shiver crawled up her spine. Susan laid her head upon her drawn-up knees and began to cry.

She knew her own mistrust was responsible for Matt's initial reluctance to share certain things about his life. Would knowing the truth about him right from the start have made any difference in how she felt about him? Swiping away at her tears, she searched for an answer. No, she realized. It wouldn't have prevented her from learning to love him.

Although Cara had assured her Matt was in no danger now, the possibility that he *could* die frightened her to the depths of her soul. He couldn't offer her any guarantees. Then again, no one could.

The thought of rejecting the happiness they could share made her future seem lonely and bleak.

Love was a risky business, she reminded herself. It simply didn't come with a warranty.

Slowly Susan's equilibrium returned. She loved him with all her heart and soul. That was the only important issue. It was a risk worth taking.

Having made her decision, she started back up the trail. Halfway back to the car, she realized she neglected to cancel her afternoon appointments. That alone should have told her where her priorities lay. She laughed for the simple joy of it.

Several weeks later Matt supervised Heath and a couple of his brawny pals in setting up a big-screen TV in the country club dining room. "A little more to the right, guys." He looked over his shoulder at Susan, who stood at the back of the room. "Can you see it okay from there?" She nodded. "That's it, then. Perfect. Thanks for the help."

Heath came over and swiped a big paw at Matt's shoulder. "Don't look so worried, buddy. The board of directors approved your promotional film. Showing it to the rest of the chamber of commerce is just a formality." A smile twitched his lips. "As a matter of fact, I think everybody's going to be . . . ah, very surprised. Wanna beer before this shindig gets going?"

Matt shook his head. He never drank to calm jangled nerves, but he wondered if maybe he should this night. The cold, calculating feeling he'd relied on in past business dealings was absent. It used to be there at his command, as much a part of him as his favorite blue power suit, white shirt, and conservatively patterned red tie. He was more nervous about this venture than he'd ever been over a multimillion-dollar computer contract. It was a strange feeling. Heath's booming voice abruptly ended his musing.

"Lord, Susie-Q, don't you look fine tonight."

Glancing toward the bar, Matt saw Heath heading for Susan. She did look exquisite, he thought proudly. Her honey-colored hair was swept up in a French twist, showing off a swirl of silver earrings. A white silk camisole lent her black evening suit a sexier than classic appeal.

His jaw clenched. Tonight he intended to put an end to her waiting game. A man had only so much patience. She was pushing his to the limit, had been since the day she'd discovered his secrets.

He had few regrets about the things he'd done in his life, but not being completely straightforward with Susan from the start was one of them. Stubborn pride had prevented him from telling her about the lucrative career he'd given up. His ego had demanded she accept him for who he was now, not who he had been. He also knew he'd kept the secret of his arrhythmia from her not, as he'd told himself, for fear she wouldn't want to get involved with him, but that she'd see him as less than a whole man.

He'd called all over town to find her that day, but no one had seen her. Then that evening she'd calmly shown up at his house for dinner with her family in tow, and she had acted as if nothing had happened. She'd dismissed with kisses his attempts to discuss his health problem and former life, and promised to take care of him. She was loving and oversolicitous to such a point, he'd come close to wanting to strangle her. When he asked if she'd reached a decision about marrying him, she told him to be patient for a little while longer. Then she asked to borrow his video camera.

He didn't know what the hell she was up to. But one way or the other, he vowed, he would have an answer from her that night.

Matt sat at the head table with the chamber of commerce officers, their spouses, and various town dignitaries. Dinner was winding down. On his left Susan held a sparkling conversation with the mayor over dessert and coffee.

"You going to eat your cheesecake?" Heath asked wistfully.

Matt grinned and passed it to him. Although the prime rib had been deliciously tender, he'd barely touched it. Heath had polished it off for him, along with whatever he could beg, borrow, or sneak off his wife's plate.

At last Web Springfield, the chamber of commerce president, rose and walked to the podium. He waited until the room quieted. "Welcome to the annual awards banquet," he began. After a short speech he introduced the various award winners.

It was almost time for the video, Matt thought. He sought Susan's hand. She gave him a brilliant smile. He smiled back, amazed at the feeling of comfort she gave him. Confidence in him shone in her eyes.

"And last, but not least," he heard the president say, "it is my great pleasure to announce Millers Creek's Citizen-of-the-Year Award. This year the award goes to a newcomer who has made a tremendous contribution to our community—Matt Martinelli, owner of Reel to Real." Web led the crowd in deafening applause.

Stunned, Matt looked blankly around the sea of faces. One by one, people rose, giving him a standing ovation. Slowly, he realized what had just happened.

Susan nudged him. "Congratulations. Go claim your award."

He stood up. Still trying to take it in, he shook hands with the president. Web presented him with a brass plaque. For a moment, all he could do was stare at the words.

Matt Martinelli, Citizen of the Year

He stepped up to the microphone. Everyone sat down again. He gazed at the people he'd come to know and care about, and for the first time, Matt felt a part of something, something greater than himself. A lump formed in his throat. He took a sustaining breath.

"I am honored to be named Millers Creek's citizen of the year. More important, I am proud to be a member of this fine community. In my travels I have spent a great deal of time in some of the most beautiful and exotic places on earth. Yet there's nowhere I would rather call home than Millers Creek.

"In the promotion film you will see this evening, I tried to capture the essence of our community. It goes without saying, we have much to offer new enterprises in the way of land, natural resources, and financial rewards. However, the businesses we hope to attract are made up of people who are just as concerned with the education, health, and welfare of their families as we are. In that respect, we have even more to offer. I—" Smiling, he waited for the renewed applause to die down.

"I thank you for your friendship, for making me feel a part of this community, and for bestowing this award upon me, undeserving as I may be. Thank you."

Feeling more happy and content than he could ever remember being before, Matt sat down while the crowd gave him another standing ovation.

Susan smiled at him. "Face it," she whispered, "you're family now, like it or not."

He picked up her hand and kissed it. "Am I going to be a part of your family?"

Her smile widened. "I'm thinking about it. Quiet. They're introducing your film. Heath just got up to put the cassette into the VCR."

He turned his attention to the wide-screen TV as someone dimmed the lights. Then he froze as a title, written in red crayon, appeared.

SUSAN LOVES MATT

After a moment's silence, laughter fluttered around the room.

"What the hell?" he whispered, almost shooting out of his chair. Several people shushed him. Slightly abashed, he settled back down and glanced at Susan. Her gaze was serenely fixed on the TV. Wondering what she was up to, he too, looked at the screen.

Susan strolled down Main Street. She was dressed in her no-nonsense black and white business suit. She held her briefcase in one hand, a clipboard in the other. The camera panned to her black low-heeled pumps clicking against the sidewalk, then lifted to her face when she stopped walking.

"Excuse me," she said to a pedestrian. It was Reesa Dunbar. "I'm doing a survey. Would you mind answering a few questions?"

"Not at all," Reesa said, waving at the person behind the camera.

"Do you know Matt Martinelli?"

"Yes."

"What do you think of him?"

"He's a very nice person."

"Do you think I should marry him?"

"Yes."

Reesa and Susan parted company.

An old farmer in overalls came by. Susan requested his help with her survey.

"Do you know Matt Martinelli?"

He scrunched up his deeply lined face. "Is he the feller what owns the video store?"

"Yes, sir. What do you think of him?"

"Well, I reckon he's okay fer a Yankee. Got the good sense to stock lots of Clint Eastwood movies in his store."

"Do you think I should marry him?"

The farmer lifted his baseball cap to scratch his head. "I met lots of those eye-talian boys when I was stationed over there during WW II. They seemed like real family folks to me." He shrugged. "You could do worse, I reckon."

Susan walked into Fred Kendall's flower shop. Fred and Martha looked the picture of American Gothic in their Sunday best, standing stiffly behind the counter, smiles painted on their faces. Susan asked them the same questions. When she came to the last one, Martha piped up, "By all means, put that poor boy out of his misery. If I was a few years younger and he were a few years older, I'd give you a run for your money, young lady!"

Fred guffawed and slapped the counter. "And ya'd still be too old, woman! Everybody knows you lie about your age."

The audience howled. Matt laughed with them.

Then came Nikki. She made her dancing debut with a snazzy jazz number while rambling on about why Matt would make a great dad.

Dellie placed her ultimate stamp of approval on him with the statement that he was turning out to have quite a green thumb in the garden.

Back out on Main Street Susan gazed thoughtfully

into the camera. A slow smile spread across her face. She walked into the shoe store. When she came out a moment later, she marched over to a city sanitation truck parked on the street. She tossed her pumps and briefcase in the back. The camera panned downward. On her feet were a pair of screaming yellow high-top sneakers patterned with a wild neon geometric design.

Somebody in the audience gave a wolf whistle. Others chuckled.

The scene switched to the high school football field. The marching band played "Yellow Submarine" for the short-skirted dance team. In line formation, the dance team flipped up cardboard signs one by one, each with a word printed on it.

MATT, WILL YOU MARRY ME? LOVE, SUSAN.

The screen went dark. Someone turned up the lights. Matt discovered every person in the room staring at him. He could practically feel them all holding their breath. He glanced at Susan. She was watching him closely. The love in her smile warmed him.

"Don't just sit there like a lump, boy," he heard Fred yell. "Kiss 'er."

Matt grinned. The grin turned into a roar of laughter that was echoed throughout the room.

It was the social event of the year. If those folks lucky enough to be invited thought it odd to hold a wedding on the riverbank, they kept it to themselves, eagerly accepted the invitation, and prayed for good weather. A sigh of relief went through the town when their prayers were answered in the form of a hot, sunny day on the Fourth of July. All two hundred people complied with the quirky dress requirements: formal dress, black tie, and sneakers.

The groom was impeccable in his black tux, pleated white shirt, black tie, and two-toned Converse high-tops. He stood straight and solemn, holding his bride's hand.

The bride was beautiful. She wore something old: her great grandmother's wedding dress, which was a confection of satin and lace. Something new: a cascading veil attached to a crown of flowers. Something borrowed: Dellie's string of pearls. And something electric blue: a pair of sneakers that had been a gift from her husband-to-be. As she joined Matt in front of the minister, Susan smiled up at him. He gazed into her eyes, which were the color of a quiet sea, and squeezed her hand.

Fred the florist beamed at his handiwork under which the happy couple stood. The white latticework arch with red roses, baby's breath, and ivy lent just the right touch. Too bad, he thought, they'd scotched Martha's plan to turn loose a dozen white doves after the minister pronounced them man and wife. Now, that would have been a real sight. He consoled himself with the thought of the fireworks that would follow the ceremony.

The bride's maid of honor cast a loving glance at her fiancé, the best man. Scott returned Reesa's gaze with a smile, knowing she was thinking of their own wedding in October.

Cara O'Mally's heart swelled with happiness for her brother. At last, he'd come home. She looked up at her husband. The giant teddy bear of a man was a sentimental softy. He had tears in his eyes. She put her arms around his waist and hugged him.

Myrtle Cooper cried loudly and joyously through the entire ceremony. Her employer's wife patted her shoulder. Old Bill Walker murmured that he'd give her a raise if she'd stop that awful caterwauling. She ignored him and boohooed to her heart's content.

Dellie had never looked more serene and regal. A new light sparkled in her blue-gray eyes. This time it is right, she thought. This time her darling girl had found a love to last forever.

She peeked at the dignified silver-haired gentleman standing beside her. Mr. Taylor wore a red rose in his lapel in place of his usual white one. A smile curved Dellie's lips. In his quiet way, Ray Taylor had been chasing after her for years. As if feeling her gaze upon him, he turned his head and winked at her. She winked back. Perhaps, she thought with delight, it was about time she let the old goat catch her.

Nikki's feet itched to dance. She was so happy inside, she could burst like a big water-filled balloon. A giggle bubbled up in her throat as she imagined the balloon going *pop* and her happiness spewing out over the crowd.

A real dad! she mouthed in silent awe. Hurry, hurry, hurry, she wanted to shout at the minister.

Soon another of her birthday wishes would officially come true. She'd made three wishes on her birthday: a dog, a dad, and a baby brother. Two out of three wasn't bad, she decided. For now. While she was waiting for the baby brother, she'd just have to console herself with movies from her dad's video store. She'd get Mom and Dad to watch all the movies that had babies in them. If they didn't get the hint, she planned to sit them down for a little family conference.

THE EDITOR'S CORNER

And what is so rare as a day in June?
Then, if ever, come perfect days . . .

With apologies to James Russell Lowell I believe we can add *and perfect reading, too,* from LOVESWEPT and FANFARE . . .

As fresh and beautiful as the rose in its title SAN ANTONIO ROSE, LOVESWEPT #474, by Fran Baker is a thrilling way to start your romance reading next month. Rafe Martinez betrayed Jeannie Crane, but her desire still burned for the only man she'd ever loved, the only man who'd ever made love to her. Rafe was back and admitting to her that her own father had driven him away. When he learned her secret, Rafe had a sure-fire way to get revenge . . . but would he? And could Jeannie ever find a way to tame the maverick who still drove her wild with ecstasy? This unforgettable love story will leave you breathless. . . .

Perfect in its powerful emotion is TOUGH GUY, SAVVY LADY, LOVESWEPT #475, by Charlotte Hughes. Charlotte tells a marvelous story of overwhelming love and stunning self-discovery in this tale of beautiful Honey Buchannan and Lucas McKay. Lucas smothered her with his love, sweetly dominating her life—and when she leaves he is distraught, but determined to win her back. Lucas has always hidden his own fears—he's a man who has pulled himself up by his boot straps to gain fortune and position—but to recapture the woman who is his life, he is going to have to change. TOUGH GUY, SAVVY LADY will touch you deeply . . . and joyfully.

Little could be so rare as being trapped IN A GOLDEN WEB, Courtney Henke's LOVESWEPT #476. Heroine Elizabeth Hammer is desperate! Framed for a crime she didn't commit, she's driven to actions she never dreamed she was capable of taking. And kidnapping gorgeous hunk Dexter Wolffe and forcing him to take her to Phoenix is just the start. Dex plays along—finding the beautiful bank manager the most delectable adversary he's ever encountered. He wants to kiss her defiant mouth and make her his prisoner . . . of love. You'll thrill to the romance of these two loners on the lam in one of LOVESWEPT's most delightful offerings ever!

And a dozen American beauties to Glenna McReynolds for her fabulously inventive OUTLAW CARSON, LOVESWEPT #478. We'll wager you've never run into a hero like Kit Carson before. Heroine Kristine Richards certainly hasn't. When the elusive, legendary Kit shows up at her university, Kristine can only wonder if he's a smuggler, a scholar—or a blessing from heaven, sent to shatter her senses. Kit is shocked by Kristine . . . for he had never believed before meeting her that there was any woman on earth who could arouse in him such fierce hunger . . . or such desperate jealousy. Both are burdened with secrets and wary of each other and have a long and difficult labyrinth to struggle through. But there are glimpses ahead of a Shangri-la just for them! As dramatic and surprising as a budding rose in winter, OUTLAW CARSON will enchant you!

Welcome to Tonya Wood who makes her debut with us with a real charmer in LOVESWEPT #477, GORGEOUS. Sam Christie was just too good-looking to be real. And too talented. And women were always throwing themselves at him. Well, until Mercy Rose Sullivan appeared in his life. When Mercy rescues Sam from the elevator in their apartment building, he can't believe what an endearing gypsy she is—or that she doesn't recognize him! Mercy is as feisty as she is guileless and puts up a terrific fight against Sam's long, slow, deep kisses. His fame is driving them apart just as love is bursting into full bloom . . . and it seems that only a miracle can bring these two dreamers together, where they belong. Sheer magical romance!

What is more perfect to read about on a perfect day than a long, lean, mean deputy sheriff and a lady locksmith who's been called to free him from the bed he is handcuffed to? Nothing! So run to pick-up your copy of SILVER BRACELETS, LOVE-SWEPT #479, by Sandra Chastain. You'll laugh and cry and root for these two unlikely lovers to get together. Sarah Wilson is as tenderhearted as they come. Asa Canyon is one rough, tough hombre who has always been determined to stay free of emotional entanglements. They taste ecstasy together . . . but is Sarah brave enough to risk loving such a man? And can Asa dare to believe that a woman will always be there for him? A romance as vivid and fresh and thrilling as a crimson rose!

And don't forget FANFARE next month with its irresistible longer fiction.

First, STORM WINDS by Iris Johansen. This thrilling, sweeping novel set against the turbulent times of the French Revolution continues with stories of those whose lives are touched by the fabled Wind Dancer. Two unforgettable pairs of lovers will have you singing the praises of Iris Johansen all summer long! DREAMS TO KEEP by Nomi Berger is a powerfully moving novel of a memorable and courageous woman, a survivor of the Warsaw ghetto, who defies all odds and builds a life and a fortune in America. But she is a woman who will risk everything for revenge on the man who condemned her family . . . until a love that is larger than life itself gives her a vision of a future of which she'd never dreamed. And all you LOVESWEPT readers will know you have to be sure to get a copy of MAGIC by Tami Hoag in which the fourth of the "fearsome foursome" gets a love for all time. This utterly enchanting love story shows off the best of Tami Hoag! Remember, FANFARE signals that something great is coming. . . .

Enjoy your perfect days to come with perfect reading from LOVESWEPT and FANFARE!

With every good wish,

Carolyn Nichols

Carolyn Nichols
Editor
LOVESWEPT
Bantam Books
666 Fifth Avenue
New York, NY 10103